Praise for Sharon Kendrick
from *Romantic Times*:

About *Getting Even:*
"Sharon Kendrick bursts with strong sexual
chemistry to enhance an unforgettable premise,
engaging scenes and substantive characters."

About *Seduced by the Boss:*
"Sharon Kendrick pens a highly charged
story with volatile characters and an
interesting twist on a fan-favorite plot."

About *Kiss and Tell:*
"Sharon Kendrick delivers a powerful story
of revenge with a gripping premise,
vibrant characters and a strong conflict...."

GREEK TYCOONS

**They're the men who have everything—
except a bride...**

Wealth, power, charm—
what else could a handsome tycoon need?
In THE GREEK TYCOONS miniseries you
have already met some gorgeous Greek
multimillionaires who are in need of wives.

Now it's the turn of popular
Presents® author Sharon Kendrick,
with her unforgettable and passionate romance
The Greek's Secret Passion

This tycoon has met his match, and he's decided
he *has* to have her...*whatever* that takes!

Sharon Kendrick

THE GREEK'S SECRET PASSION

GREEK
TYCOONS

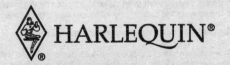

HARLEQUIN®

TORONTO • NEW YORK • LONDON
AMSTERDAM • PARIS • SYDNEY • HAMBURG
STOCKHOLM • ATHENS • TOKYO • MILAN • MADRID
PRAGUE • WARSAW • BUDAPEST • AUCKLAND

For the man with the commanding presence.
He knows who he is.

ISBN 0-373-12345-0

THE GREEK'S SECRET PASSION

First North American Publication 2003.

This edition published by arrangement with Harlequin Books S.A.

® and TM are trademarks of the publisher. Trademarks indicated with
® are registered in the United States Patent and Trademark Office, the
Canadian Trade Marks Office and in other countries.

Visit us at www.eHarlequin.com

Printed in U.S.A.

CHAPTER ONE

A MAN'S voice flowed over the air like warm, sweet honey and something about its lazy caress had Molly putting her pen down and staring blankly at the open window.

'Nato, Zoe,' said the voice again. *'Maressi!'*

A Greek voice. Unmistakably. Soft and sexy and deep.

Little sizzles of awareness pricked at her skin until Molly deliberately sent them packing. Having a Greek lover a lifetime ago didn't mean you had to have an attack of the vapours every time you heard one of his compatriots speak, surely? The pang she felt was instinctive but only momentary, and she picked up her pen again.

Then she heard the voice again, only this time it was laughing and this time she froze.

For a laugh was something unique, wasn't it? Voices changed and some voices mimicked others you had heard—but a laugh. Oh, no. A laugh was different and this one took her right back to a place which was out of bounds.

She walked over to the window with a heart which was beating far too fast for the sight of something which would surely mock her and tell her that she was being a sentimental fool.

But the rich ebony hair of the man who hoisted a case out of the car with such ease did little to reassure her that her thoughts had been of the mad, ridiculous variety. Yet what had she been expecting—that the owner of the voice would be blond? Because if the man was Greek—as he surely was—then, of course he would have coal dark hair and olive skin and the kind of strength which few men she encountered these days seemed to have.

He slammed the car door shut, and, almost as if he sensed he was being watched, he began to lift his head towards the house and Molly hastily withdrew from the window. What kind of impression would *that* create? A stereotype of the nosy neighbour busy twitching behind a curtain to see just what kind of family the latest house-let would yield.

But a vague sense of disquiet kept her heart racing as she heard the front door of the adjoining house close, and when she went to pick up her pen again she noticed that her fingers were trembling.

Forget it, she told herself. Or put your mind at rest.

Later, she decided as she began to make notes— she would do just that.

Dimitri put the bag down in the hall as his daughter began exclaiming about the high ceilings, the huge windows and the view from the back onto a dream of an English garden. He smiled. 'It is a good house, yes?'

'Oh, it's a *wonderful* house, Papa!'

'You want to go and choose your room?'

Zoe pulled a mock-shocked face. 'Any room I like?'

Dimitri flashed her an indulgent smile, which briefly softened the hard, stark lines of his dark face. 'Any room you like,' he agreed equably, glancing idly through a pile of mail which had been left stacked on the table in the hall. Mostly bills and circulars—and one large and expensive white envelope addressed, 'To the New Residents!'

His lips curved and he put the whole stack down, unopened, then spent an hour unpacking—shifting silk and linen into various cupboards and drawers with the kind of automatic efficiency which evolved after frequent trips abroad. He had just set up his computer on a desk in the room he intended to use as an office, when the front door bell rang, and he frowned.

None of his business contacts would come here. He had a couple of friends in the city, but he had planned to give them a call once he was settled. Which left, he guessed, a neighbour—for who else could it be, other than someone from one of the adjoining houses, who must have seen them arrive?

He sincerely hoped that this was not the first in a long deputation of well-wishers—though maybe that was wishful thinking on his part. Nothing came without a cost and he had deliberately chosen the house in a residential area, mainly for Zoe's sake. Neighbours promised an element of security and safety and normality which you didn't get in hotels—

but the downside to neighbours was a tendency to intrude, to try to get close.

And Dimitri Nicharos didn't allow anyone to get close.

He went downstairs and opened the door with a cool smile, preparing to say hello and goodbye in quick succession. But the smile died on his lips and something unknown and forgotten stirred into life as he stared at the tall blonde woman who was standing on his doorstep, a bottle of wine held in her hand and an incredulous expression on her face which made her look as if she had seen some terrible ghost.

It took a moment or two for it to dawn on him just exactly what—or who—it was he was seeing and, when it did, he felt the same kind of incredulity which had made the woman's luscious lips part into a disbelieving 'O', but he kept his own face calm and impassive. He needed time to think, to assimilate the facts, and he would not be seen to react. He had learned that. He never let anyone know what he was thinking, for knowledge was power, and he liked to hold the balance to favour him.

He stared at her. 'Hello,' he said softly, as if he was talking to a complete stranger. But she was, wasn't she? And maybe she always had been.

Molly stared back, her breathing rapid and shallow. It was like suddenly finding yourself on the top of a mountain, without realising that you had been climbing. She felt faint. From shock. From disbelief. And just from the sheer overriding awareness that, yes, this was Dimitri. Her fantasy on hearing the rich, deep laugh had not been fantasy at all. A man from the past—*the* man from her past—was here, and exuding that same lethal brand of sexual charisma which had once so ensnared her. It was ensnaring her now, for all she could do was to greedily drink in the sight of him, like a woman who had been starved of men all her life.

His skin was glowing and golden, with eyes dark as olives, framed by lashes thick as pine forests. He had filled out, of course—but not in the way that so many men in their mid-thirties had. There was no paunch hanging over the edge of his belt, nor any fleshy folds of skin around his chin denoting an indolent lifestyle with not enough attention paid to exercise. No, Dimitri was sheer, honed muscle, the pale linen trousers and cool silk shirt emphasising every hard sinew of his body.

True, the black hair was less unruly than before and there was a touch of silver at the temples, but the mouth was exactly as she remembered it—and, boy, did she remember it—a cushioned, sensual mouth which looked as though it had been designed purely for a woman's pleasure.

But the eyes. Oh, the eyes. There was the difference, the one big, tell-tale difference. Once they had shone at her with, not love, no—though she had prayed for that—but with a fierce, possessive affection.

Today these eyes were as coldly glittering as jet. They gave nothing away, and expected nothing in return.

She drew a deep breath from dry lungs which felt as though they had been scorched from within. 'Dimitri?' she managed. 'Is it really you?'

Dimitri raised his eyebrows in question, enjoying her discomfiture, almost as much as he was enjoying looking at her. But then he always had. Women like Molly Garcia were rare. Physical perfection—or as close to it as you would find in one lifetime. An irresistible combination of hair that was moon-pale and streaked with sunshine—and eyes so icy-blue that they should have been cold, yet he had seen them hotter than hot and on fire with need and desire.

Deliberately taking his time to answer a question which was as unnecessary as it was pointless, he let his eyes drift slowly over her body. And what a body. Still. Even though that body had inevitably changed during the journey from teenager to woman. Back then she had been as slender as a young lemon sapling, so slender that sometimes he had feared she might break when he made love to her—but now she bore the firm curves of a fruit-bearing tree. Her hips were still slender, but her breasts were rich and ripe and lush and Dimitri had to work hard at appearing impassive, only just succeeding in keeping the studied look of indifference on his face. His body he had less control over.

'Perhaps I have acquired an identical twin brother?' he mocked. 'What do you think?'

Part of her had been hoping that it was all some kind of mistake, even while the other part had prayed for it not to be so, but any lingering doubt fled just as soon as he began to speak, with that heady mixture of deep, honeyed emphasis she remembered all too well.

She could do one of two things. She could stand there, gaping at him like a fish which had suddenly been starved of water, or she could be herself—the bright, successful and independent woman she had become.

She smiled, even though her mouth felt as though she were stretching a coat-hanger through a jar of glue. 'Good heavens!' she exclaimed, with just the right amount of amused surprise. 'I can't believe it!'

'I can hardly believe it myself,' he murmured, thinking that this was fevered fantasy brought to life. His eyes strayed to her fingers. No wedding band. Did that mean that she was free? *Available?* 'It's been a long time.'

Too long, and yet not long enough—for surely time should have gone some way towards protecting her from his sensual impact. So why had time failed her? Why did she find herself feeling overwhelmed with weakness when confronted with the sight of her former Greek lover? She sucked in a dry breath as memories of him pressing her naked body against the soft sand washed over her.

'What on earth are you doing here?' she demanded.

'I am staying here.'

'Why?'

But before he could reply, she heard the sound of a voice speaking in Greek. A woman's voice. And reality shot home. Of course he had a woman with him. Probably children, too. Large houses in this part of London were let to families, and he had doubtless brought his with him.

It was no more than she had expected, so why did it hurt so much?

And then she stared in a kind of disbelieving daze as the most beautiful creature she had ever seen came loping down the stairs towards them.

Glossy black hair cascaded down over high, pert breasts—her jeans and T-shirt showing off a slim, boyish figure and emphasising legs which seemed to go on and on forever. Her face was a perfect opal, with deep-set black eyes which dominated it and a luscious, smiling mouth.

And Molly's determination not to appear fazed almost failed her as the woman grew closer—why, she looked almost young enough to be... Her forced smile faded from her lips. Had he become one of those men who paraded a female on his arm who was young enough to be his daughter?

'Papa?'

She *was* his daughter.

Molly found herself doing rapid sums inside her head while Dimitri answered the girl in Greek. She looked seventeen—maybe eighteen—but that would mean...that would mean... She shook her head. She didn't understand. For that would mean that Dimitri had had a daughter when he had known *her*. And surely that was not possible? Or had she been so wrong about so many things?

Suddenly, she felt faint, wishing that she could just disappear, but how could she? Instead she stood there like some dumb fool with a bottle of wine in her hand, the last of her youthful dreams shattering as the teenager approached them.

Rather reluctantly, Dimitri spoke. He had been rather enjoying the play of emotions across her lovely face, which Molly had desperately been trying to hide. This was indeed a unique situation, and the novelty factor of that for a man like Dimitri was almost as enjoyable as the sight of Molly Garcia looking so helpless.

'Zoe!' He smiled. 'We have a visitor.' And the black eyes were turned to Molly in mocking question. Over to you, the look seemed to say, unhelpfully.

Speaking was proving even more difficult than it had been before. 'I live next door,' said Molly quickly. 'I, er—I saw you arrive, and I thought I would bring you this…to welcome you. Welcome,' she finished. She held up the bottle with a grimace, but the girl smiled widely and took it from Molly, casting an admonishing little look at her father.

'How very kind of you,' she said, in softly accented English. 'Please—you will come in?'

Like hell she would! 'No, no, honestly—'

'Oh, do. Please,' said Dimitri, in a silky voice. 'I insist.'

She met his eyes and saw the mischief and mockery there. How dared he? Didn't he have a single ounce of perception? Didn't he realise that she might actually find it difficult to meet his wife? Though why should he, when she stopped to think about it? Maybe this unusual situation was not so unusual for a man like Dimitri. How many other women were there like her, dotted around the place—never quite able to forget his sweet, sensual skills?

And she noticed that he hadn't introduced her. Did that mean he had *forgotten her name*? Nor had he told his daughter that they had once known each other—though maybe that wasn't so surprising, either. For what would he say?

Molly and I were lovers.

Put like that, it sounded nothing, but it *had* been something—it *had*. Or had she just been fooling herself all these years that her first love had been special and had just ended badly? And just how old *was* his daughter? Even if she was younger than she looked that still meant that he must have fathered her just after Molly had left the tiny island....

She couldn't think straight.

And maybe that was why she felt as if setting foot inside the door would be on a par with entering the lion's den. Some memories were best left untouched. Parts of the past were cherished, and maybe they only stayed that way if you didn't let the present intrude on them.

She shook her head, mocking him back with a meaningless smile of her own. 'It is very kind of you, but I'm afraid that I have work to do.'

He glanced at the expensive gold timepiece on his

hair-roughened wrist. 'At four o'clock?' he questioned mildly. 'You work shifts?'

Did he still think she was a waitress, then? 'I work from home,' she explained, then wished she hadn't, for a dark gleam of interest lightened the black eyes and suddenly she felt vulnerable.

'Please,' said the girl, and held her hand out. 'You must think us very rude. I am Zoe Nicharos—and this is my father, Dimitri.'

'Molly,' she said back, for what choice did she have? 'Molly Garcia.' She shook Zoe's hand and let it go, but then Dimitri reached out and, with an odd kind of smile, took her fingers and clasped them inside the palm of his hand.

Outwardly, it was nothing more than a casual handshake but she could feel the latent strength in him and her skin stirred with a kind of startled recognition, as if this was what a man's touch *should* be like.

'Hello, *Molly*,' he murmured. 'I'm Dimitri.'

Just the way he said it made her stomach melt, despite him, despite everything and she wondered if he could feel the sudden acceleration of her heart. She tried to prise her fingers away, but he wouldn't let her, not until she had met his amused black gaze full-on, and she realised that she was the one who was affected by all this—and that Dimitri was simply taking some kind of faintly amused pleasure in it all. As if it were some kind of new spectator sport. As if it didn't matter—and why should it? She should be flattered that he remembered her at all.

Her smile felt more practised now; she was getting quite good at this. 'Well, like I said—this was just a brief call to welcome you. I hope you'll all be very happy here,' she said.

He heard the assumption in the word 'all', but he let it go. This was going to be interesting, he thought. *Very* interesting. 'I'm sure we will,' he answered, with a smooth, practised smile of his own. His eyes lingered briefly on the swell of her breasts, outlined like two soft peaches by a pale blue silk shirt which matched her eyes. 'It's a very beautiful place.'

It had been a long time since a man had looked at her that way and she felt the slow, heavy pulsing of awareness—as if her body had been in a deep, deep sleep and just one glittering black stare had managed to stir it into life again. She had to get away before he realised that, unless, of course, he already had.

'I really must go,' she said.

'Thank you for the wine,' he said softly. 'Maybe some time…when you're not so busy *working*…you might come round and have a drink with us?'

'Maybe,' she said brightly, but they both knew that she was lying.

CHAPTER TWO

MOLLY let herself into her house, trying to tell herself not to overreact. It was something that was nothing—just something which occurred time and time again. And that the only reason this had never happened before was because they lived in different worlds.

She had come face to face with a man she'd once been in love with, that was all—though a more cynical person might simply describe it as teenager lust and infatuation. Her Greek-island lover had materialised with his family in the house next door to hers, and it was nothing more than an incredible coincidence.

And not so terrible, surely?

But the thought of just going upstairs and carrying on with her research notes was about as attractive as the idea of putting on a bikini to sunbathe in the back garden, wondering if everything she did now would be visible to Dimitri's eyes. And telling herself that, even if it was, she shouldn't care. These things happened in a grown-up world and she was going to have to face it.

Just as she was going to have to face his wife—and though the thought of that had no earthly right to hurt her, it did.

She went through the motions of normality. She met a friend for a drink and then went to see a film. And spent a night waking over and over, to find that the bright red numbers on her digital clock had only moved on by a few minutes.

She showered and dressed and made coffee, and when the doorbell rang she bit her lip, telling herself that it was only the postman, but she knew it was not the postman. Call it sixth sense or call it feminine intuition, but she knew exactly who would be standing on her doorstep.

And he was.

She opened the door and stared into the black, enigmatic eyes.

'Dimitri,' she offered warily.

'Molly,' he mimicked, mocking her wary tone. 'I am disturbing you?'

He couldn't do anything but disturb her, but she shook her head. 'Not really.'

'You aren't working?' He raised his eyebrows.

'Not at the moment, no.' She answered the question in his eyes. 'I write,' she explained.

'Novels?'

She shook her head. 'Travel books, and articles, actually, but that's really beside the point. Look, Dimitri—I don't know what it is you want—I'm just a little surprised to see you here.'

His eyes mocked her. 'But you knew I would come.'

Yes. She had known that. 'Was there something particular you wanted?'

'Don't you think we need to talk?'

'To say what?'

'Oh, come on, Molly,' he chided softly. 'There's more than a little unfinished business between us, *ne*? Do you think we can just ignore the past, as though it never happened? Pass each other by in the street, like polite strangers?'

'Why not?'

'Because life doesn't work like that.'

'No.' She wondered if his wife knew he was here, but that was his business, not hers. And he was right—there *was* unfinished business. Things that had never been said that maybe should be, especially if she was going to be bumping into him all over the place. 'I guess you'd better come in, then.' Her voice sounded cool as she said it, but inside she felt anything but.

'Thank you,' he murmured.

He hadn't expected it to be so easy, though maybe he should have done if he had stopped to think about it. For hadn't it always been too deliciously easy with her? Such a seamless seduction it had been with Molly, and hadn't there been some perverse, chauvinistic streak in him which wished she had put up more of a fight?

He observed the polite, glacial smile—thinking that there was a coolness about her now, which might suggest something else. That she didn't give a damn whether she spoke to him or not. Or that there was another man in her life—for surely someone as beautiful as Molly would not be alone?

Another man whom she adored as once she had said she adored him.

He stepped inside, and the pert, high thrust of her buttocks hit some powerful button in his memory. He felt a pulse begin to throb deep and strong within his groin and his body felt as though it had betrayed him. She moved with a confident assurance, and something about this new, older Molly set his loins melting in a way which both frustrated and infuriated him.

He had known her one long, hot summer on Pondiki—a summer of thoughtless passion. She had driven him and every other hot-blooded man on the island insane with desire that summer. Those tiny little cotton dresses she had worn when she had been working. Or outrageous scraps of material only just covering her body on the beach. Or naked as could be, with just the darkened circles of her nipples and the faint fuzz of hair at her thighs—the only things breaking up the smoothness of that bare, pale flesh.

He had triumphed in the joy of knowing that only *he* had seen her undressed and uninhibited like that, but in that he had been wrong. And he had been a fool, he thought bitterly. Even now, the memory still had the power to anger him—but then it had been the first and the last time he had been betrayed by a woman.

She turned to face him, determined to present the image of the slick, urban professional, even if inside she felt like the impressionable teenager she had once been. Yesterday, she had reacted gauchely, but yesterday she had had a reason to do so. Yesterday his appearance had been like a bolt out of the blue. Today there was no excuse. 'I was just having some coffee—would you like some?'

He smiled. How times had changed. She used to practically rip the clothes from his body when she saw him. Who would have thought that one day she would be offering him coffee in a chilly, distant way he would never have associated with Molly? 'Why not?'

She felt like a stranger in her own home as he followed her into the kitchen and sat down on one of the high stools at the breakfast bar, but then Dimitri dominated his surroundings like some blazing star. He always had.

'Do you still take it black?'

He gave a careless smile. 'Ah. You remember?'

Molly's hand was shaking slightly as she poured their coffee, automatically handing him a cup of the strong brew, unsugared and untouched by milk, and he took it from her, a mocking look in his black eyes.

Oh, yes, she remembered all right. Strange that you could learn your tables and French verbs by heart for years at school and some of them would stubbornly refuse to reappear and yet you could remember almost everything about a man with whom you had enjoyed a brief, passionate affair. So was the memory selective—or just cruel?

'Don't read too much into it, Dimitri! Everyone in Greece takes their coffee that way!' she countered as she reached for a mug.

But he wondered what else she remembered. The feel of his flesh enfolding hers, the sheer power as he had driven into her, over and over again? Was she remembering that now? As he was. She had left him dazed—in a way that no woman before nor since had ever quite done—and where once he had revelled in that fact, it had afterwards come to haunt him.

She pushed the coffee towards him, hating herself for thinking that his silken skin was close enough to touch. For a long time she had yearned to have him this close again, and now that he was she felt... Briefly, Molly closed her eyes. She was *scared*, and she wasn't quite sure why. 'Here.'

'Thanks.' But he ignored the coffee and instead let his gaze drift over her.

She wore a short denim skirt and a white T-shirt which had flowers splashed across the breasts. Her feet were bare and her toenails painted a shiny cherry-pink, and he felt his mouth dry with automatic desire. Some women knew how to press a man's buttons just by existing—and Molly Garcia was one of them.

'You're staring,' she said quietly.

'Yes. I imagine that most men do.'

'Not in quite such a blatant way.'

'Ah.' He smiled. 'But I am Greek, and we are not ashamed to show our appreciation of beautiful things.'

She remembered *that*, too, and how much it had appealed to her at the time. And it wasn't just where women were concerned—it was the same with good food, a cooing baby, or a spectacular sunset—Greek men were open about showing their pleasure in the good things in life.

With an effort, he tore his eyes away from the diversions of her body, forcing his attention on the high-ceilinged room instead. 'And this is a beautiful house.'

'Yes, it is.' She forced herself to concentrate. 'But you aren't here to talk about my house.' And neither was he here to stare at her in a way that reminded her all too vividly of how close they had once been.

'No.' He was scanning the room for signs of male habitation, but there was none. None that he could see. 'You're married?'

'I was. Not any more. I'm divorced.'

'Ah.' A jerk of triumph knifed its way through him. 'There is a lot of it about.'

The way he said it made her feel guilty—or had that been his intention? She knew his views on divorce. The break-up of families. He had condemned the easy-come, easy-go way of life which had been so alien to his own. She knew what his next question would be before he asked it.

'Children?'

'No.' Molly stirred her coffee unnecessarily, then lifted her eyes to his. So far he had been the one asking all the questions, but she had a few of her own. 'Do you have any more—apart from Zoe?'

He shook his head. 'Just Zoe.'

'And your wife? Won't she think it a little strange

that you've come here this morning? Are you planning to tell her about us?'

'What "us" was that, Molly?' he retorted softly. 'What is there to tell? That we were lovers, until someone better came along?'

Someone *better*? As if anyone could be better than Dimitri!

'Someone else to lose yourself in and to vent that remarkable, newly discovered sexual hunger on?' he continued, quietly yet remorselessly. He remembered the sight of the man's bare chest. Of Molly's unbuttoned dress. Of the way that the man's hand had rested with possession over the swell of her hip, and the image had the blinding power to take him right back. To recall how he had wanted to smash his fist into something. 'Was he a good lover, Molly? As good as me?'

Even now, the sense of injustice was powerful enough to hurt her. To be wrongly judged struck at the very heart of her. And stung as she was by the need to defend herself, everything else dissolved into insignificance—for wasn't he now giving her the opportunity to tell him what he had refused to hear at the time? The truth?

'You don't really, honestly think that I had sex with James that night?'

'*James,*' he mimicked cruelly. 'Ah! I did not know his name. James.' The black eyes glittered. 'It was, of course, simply a little craziness on my part, was it not, *agape mou*—that when I find my girlfriend in bed with another man, to assume that they had been having sex? Whatever could have given me that idea? Don't forget, Molly—I knew what you were like. I knew how much you *loved* it—I have never known a woman who fell so completely and utterly in love with sex the way you did.'

What use would it serve now to qualify his accusation with the plaintive little cry that it had been *him* she had loved? And *that* had been what had made it so mind-blowingly and uniquely special. Sex with Dimitri had seemed as easy and as necessary as breathing. She could no more have been intimate with another man at that time than she could have grown wings and flown

'Had you tired of me?' he demanded. 'Was that why you took the American into your arms and into your bed? Had you taken your fill of me, Molly— eager to try out your newly acquired skills with someone different?'

But she was still filled with the burning need to separate truth from falsehood. 'I never touched him, Dimitri,' she whispered. 'Nor he me—not in the way you are thinking.'

He remembered the abandoned posture of her sprawled, bare legs. It had been the first time in his life that he had experienced real jealousy, and its potency had unsettled him. 'What way am I supposed to think? He was asleep on the bed next to you!'

'It wasn't like that!'

'*Ochi?*' He gave a slow, cruel smile. 'Then how was it? I am so interested to hear.'

'He was comforting me.'

'Comforting you?' He laughed. 'Lucky man indeed—to offer comfort in such a way! I must begin to offer comfort to beautiful women—how very noble it will make me feel!'

And suddenly Molly had had enough. He was in *her* house and this was *her* territory and yet she was allowing him to dominate in the way that came so naturally to him. Throwing accusations at her and here she was, weakly trying to defend herself—when didn't she have a few accusations of her own?

'Actually, yes, he was comforting me,' she said. She looked him straight in the face. 'Because I had just found out about Malantha, you see.'

He stilled then, became so still that an outside observer might have wondered if he breathed at all. Only the ebony glitter from the narrowed eyes showed that he did.

'What about Malantha?' he questioned softly.

'That she was the girl you were promised to! I discovered that I had been nothing but a light, summer diversion, one in just a long line of willing lovers! I saw you both together, you see, Dimitri. I discovered that night what everyone else on the island knew—that Malantha was always the girl you were intended to marry—and, yes, I was upset. Very upset,' she finished, though the word sounded tame when she said it now.

Upset? At the time it had felt as though her heart had been torn from her body and ripped apart, with the edges left raw and jagged and gaping. First love and first heartbreak—and didn't they say that the cut of first love was the deepest cut of all?

Everyone had told her that the pain would fade and eventually heal, and heal it had. It had just left a faint but indelible scar along the way.

She lifted her head and stared at him, her eyes bright and searching. 'What happened to Malantha, by the way?' she asked.

There was a pause, a pause that seemed to go on for ever and ever.

'I married her.'

The world shifted out of focus, and when it shifted back in again it looked different. It was what she had half known and half expected and yet not what she wanted to hear. For hadn't there been a foolish part of her that longed for him to tell her that she had been mistaken? That he had not been promised to Malantha at all. Or that he had, but had changed his mind along the way.

In a way it made things worse, and yet in a funny kind of way it made things better. So she had not been wrong. Those nights when she had lain awake wondering if she had ruined everything by jumping to a stupid conclusion had been wasted nights. Her instincts had been right all along.

She sucked in a dry, painful breath. 'Then hadn't you better be getting back to her?' she questioned coldly. 'In the circumstances, I doubt whether she would approve of you sitting in my kitchen, drinking my coffee—do you, Dimitri?'

'My wife is dead,' he said baldly.

There was a moment of terrible, stunned silence and Molly was rocked by emotions so basic and conflicting that for several long seconds she could not speak.

Dead? She looked at him blankly, seeking and finding the sombre affirmation in his eyes. 'I'm so sorry,' she whispered. 'W…when?' she asked ineffectually.

'When Zoe was a baby.'

'Oh, God, Dimitri—that's awful.'

He shook his head. He didn't want her sympathy. It was mistimed and irrelevant now. He wanted *her*, he realised. He always had and he still did. To lose himself in the soft white folds of her body. To feel that tumble of blonde hair swaying like silk against his chest. Desire could strike at any time, and this could not be a more inappropriate one, but that didn't stop him feeling its slow, stealthy course through his veins, like some unstoppable drug.

'It was a long time ago. It is past.'

For a moment, all that could be heard was the ticking of the clock.

'How old is Zoe now?' she asked suddenly.

The black eyes narrowed. 'Fifteen.'

This time the sums were easier. 'So you married Malantha soon after I had left?' But she didn't need an answer to that. 'Of course you did.' She looked him straight in the eye. 'Just tell me one thing, Dimitri—were you sleeping with her at the same time you were sleeping with me?'

His eyes iced over and his mouth curved with distaste. If anything could demonstrate their fundamental differences, then that one question had managed it with blinding simplicity. 'Of course not. Malantha was brought up to be a virgin on her wedding night.'

It was meant to wound, and it did—but it was the truth, and who was she to argue with that?

She wanted to tell him to drink his coffee and go, and yet wasn't there some irrational side of her that wanted the very opposite? To take him into her arms as if the intervening years simply hadn't happened— and, in the process, to exorcise him and his sensual influence once and for all.

'So now what?' she questioned, amazed at how steady her voice sounded. 'You haven't even told me why you're here, or how long you're staying. Or even how you ended up living so close?'

Her eyes were questioning and he gave a soft laugh. 'You think I tracked you down? Found where you were living and moved into the house next door?'

As he said it she realised how preposterous the idea was. 'So it's just a terrible coincidence?'

Terrible? Right at that moment, it didn't seem so terrible. The woman who had always been able to take him straight to heaven and back was living in the house next door. Thoughtfully, Dimitri stroked the pad of his thumb against the warm circumference of the coffee-cup. If fate had provided such a breath-taking opportunity for a taste of former pleasures, then who was he to refuse such an opportunity?

He stared at her, wondering if there really was such a thing as coincidence? Now that he came to think about it, hadn't she once described Hampstead to him, telling him how beautiful it was and painting a picture of the heath and all its glories? Had that description planted a seed in his subconscious mind, so that, when he had been choosing where to stay in London, he had instinctively plumped for the leafy green area which seemed so far from the centre of a city it was so close to? Had he subconsciously willed fate to step in—and had it not done just that?

'I am here for a few weeks,' he said slowly. 'Zoe is going to an English summer school and I wanted to accompany her.'

Her mind ticked over; she was getting quite good at mental arithmetic. A few weeks. It wasn't a lifetime. Surely it wouldn't take too much planning for both of them to be able to keep out of the other's way for that long. As long as they were agreed.

'So what are we going to do?'

'Do? What do you suggest?' More as a diversionary tactic, he picked up his coffee and sipped it, black eyes challenging her through the thin cloud of steam which rose up like clouds. He wondered what she would say if he told her exactly what he would like to do at that precise moment, and how she would react. Would she open her mouth to his if he pulled her into his arms and began to kiss her? He saw the inky dilation of her pupils and once again he felt the powerful pull of desire. Because nothing was more seductive than mutual desire, particularly if one of the parties was doing their utmost to suppress it. 'We are neighbours, Molly,' he said softly. 'And we must behave as neighbours do.'

'You mean…' she swallowed '…avoid each other wherever possible?'

'Is that how English neighbours behave?' he mocked. He shook his head and smiled. 'On the contrary,' he said, and the gravel-deep voice sounded as sweet as honey as he rose to his feet, managing to make the high-ceilinged kitchen look like a doll's house with his tall, dominating figure. 'We will say good morning and talk about the weather whenever we meet!'

'Ha, ha, ha,' she said automatically.

He raised his eyebrows. 'But we are both grown up now, *ne*? I have been married and you have been married. What is it that you say—about a lot of water?'

'Has flowed under the bridge,' she filled in automatically, and remembering how she had helped him with his English was curiously more poignant than anything else. She slid her legs down off the stool and wished she hadn't. She was a tall woman, but Dimitri managed to make her feel like a tiny little thing; and her skirt was suddenly feeling as though it had shrunk in the wash.

'Gallons of the stuff!' she joked, thinking that soon this would be over. It had to be. He would see sense and realise that they couldn't possibly ever be friends, and they certainly couldn't be anything else, either. Not now.

He smiled then, but it was an odd, grown-up smile

that Molly didn't recognise and it threatened her more than a smile ever should.

'So I will come to your party,' he stated softly.

She stared at him. 'My p-party? What are you talking about?'

'You are having a party, Molly.'

Had he turned into a mind-reader? Were there balloons and boxes of champagne glasses lying around the place, giving him clues? Feeling half mad and disorientated, Molly looked round the kitchen. No. 'How the hell did you know *that*?'

She wasn't thinking straight, or clearly—and there was usually only one reason why a woman acted in such a distracted way, he noted with a warm sense of triumph. 'You sent me an invitation, remember? "To The New Residents!"' he quoted drily.

Of course she had. She had posted them all the way down the road; she always did. Her heart had begun to thunder and she wasn't such a self-deluding fool as to deny that part of the reason was excitement. But it would be madness if he came. Sheer and utter madness.

'I sent an invitation to all my neighbours,' she said wildly. 'Because it'll probably be noisy, and late.'

'Well, then.' He shrugged his broad shoulders. 'You want to pacify your neighbours, of which I am one? Then pacify *me*, Molly.'

'Dimitri,' she appealed, steeling herself against the sensual undercurrent in his tone, wondering if that had been deliberate or just part of the whole irresistible package he presented. 'You can't seriously want to come?'

'Oh, but I can,' he demurred. 'It will be good for me to mix a little while I'm here, don't you think? And besides—' he gave a slow, curving smile '—I like parties.'

She bet he liked them!

'Well, of course I can't *un*invite you now,' she observed slowly. She raised her face to his with a defiant tilt to her chin, in a gesture which told him quite clearly that she could cope with his presence. She certainly wasn't going to give him the pleasure of being barred! 'So if you insist on coming, then I guess I can't stop you.'

When she lifted her face like that, she was almost begging to be kissed and the desire to do so almost took his breath away. What *would* she do if he kissed her? he wondered. 'You could stop me if you wanted to,' he taunted softly. 'You just don't want to. Do you, Molly?'

Not if she was going to show him that she didn't really care one way or the other. 'Oh, it'll be interesting to see your predatory instincts at work with my friends,' she said sweetly. She made a great pantomime of looking at her watch. 'Now I really do have things to do—shall I show you out?'

Without waiting for an answer, she marched out of the kitchen towards the hall, and, reluctantly, Dimitri began to follow her. He was being dismissed! It was behaviour that he simply would not have tolerated from another woman and he felt the dull, hot ache of frustration as she opened the door. Then allowed himself to think of the tantalising inevitability of what was going to happen between them.

He glittered her a smile.

The kiss could wait.

CHAPTER THREE

BUT after Dimitri had gone, Molly did something she had not allowed herself to do for years. She ran upstairs, to the clutter of the junk room which lay at the very top of the house. Here there were books and documents and certificates: things you told yourself you might need one day, but rarely did—yet things you didn't dare throw away, just in case.

The old leather box was dusty, packed with shells, an old charm-bracelet, a lucky four-leaf clover sellotaped to a piece of card. In here was a sentimental record of the years, and, right at the bottom, a photograph.

She pulled it out and looked at it. Her and Dimitri, frozen in time, their arms tight around each other, carefree smiles on their young faces. The only photo she had.

Visual images had the power to drag you right back, to take you to a place which you had kept firmly out of bounds, and as Molly stared in Dimitri's heartbreakingly beautiful young face she stepped right back into the past.

A holiday job on the Greek island of Pondiki had seemed like heaven to an eighteen-year-old schoolgirl in the long vacation before she went to university. One minute she was hurling her blazer across the room, the next she was stepping out onto the blistering tarmac of Pondiki's tiny runway on a high summer's day. Grown up and free—with a suitcase full of cotton dresses and bikinis and not a care in the world.

There were just three hotels on the island and at that time it was off the beaten tourist-track. Most people opted for the bigger, livelier Greek destinations, and only discerning travellers and students had discovered the unspoilt beauty of the mouse-shaped paradise, with its lemon groves and pine trees and the towering Mount Urlin which dominated it.

Molly was a waitress in one of the tavernas and she worked lunchtimes and evenings. Afternoons, she was free. The work was undemanding—though she developed strong arms from carrying trays of beer and wine—and she was given her own small, shuttered room which overlooked the main square, which at night was lit by rainbow-coloured lights. When she lay in bed, after the busy shift had ended, she could hear the sound of the waves lapping on the soft white sands and sometimes she thought she had died and gone to heaven.

She made friends with the daughter of the owner— a Greek girl named Elena who was as keen to learn English as Molly was to learn Greek.

It wasn't easy. Greek was a difficult language.

'You should get one of the boys to teach you,' ventured Elena shyly.

Molly wrinkled her nose. 'I'm not into boys,' she said.

It was true; she wasn't. She had no interest in the youths whose dark eyes followed her as she walked across the sunlit square in a cotton dress, with a straw sunhat to protect the blonde hair which seemed to fascinate them.

And then she met Dimitri and suddenly everything changed.

She and Elena had borrowed a scooter and ridden round to the opposite side of the island, where Pondiki's most exclusive hotel lay sheltered in splendid isolation, and they had just sputtered to a halt when they heard an angry shout, and as Molly had turned around her heart had turned over.

She fell in love with him right there and then, it was as simple as that. She didn't know why or how she knew it, she just did.

It wasn't just because he seemed like a man, and not a boy—though he was only a few months older than her. Nor because his dark good looks made him look like some kind of diabolical angel. Nor the fact that his hard brown torso was bare and he wore just faded denims which clung to the narrow jut of his hips and his long, muscular legs.

It was something in his eyes. Something indefinable in the look he directed at her. It was a look which her upbringing should have made her rebel against. A swift, assessing look. Almost judgemental. But it made her feel as if she had come home—as if she had spent all her life seeking just that look.

Except that, for now, it was a very angry look.

And it was only afterwards that she discovered he made every English girl who visited Pondiki feel the same way, but by then it was too late. If only someone had told her—yet if they had, would she have listened?

'Who *is* that?' she whispered.

'It is Dimitri,' whispered Elena, as if indeed it really *were* the devil himself.

'Dimitri who?'

But Elena shook her head, because he was striding towards them. He completely ignored Molly and let out a torrent of furious Greek which was directed solely at Elena.

Molly listened uncomprehendingly for a moment or two. 'What's the problem?'

Dimitri stopped speaking and turned to look at her, his heart beating fast, and it was more than his usual instinctive and hot-blooded reaction to a beautiful blonde. She was English. He had heard about her, of course, but he had been too busy helping his father to go looking for himself, and this was the first time he had seen her.

He was Greek through and through and he loved beautiful women. He took and enjoyed what was on offer, but it lasted only as long as his interest—which was never long.

Yet there was something indefinably different about this woman. A goddess of a woman, her icy-blue eyes almost on a level with his own, with a beauty he found almost overwhelming. But he saw the returning spark of interest in *her* eyes and this normal state of play was enough to allow his naturally arrogant masculine superiority to reassert itself.

'Are you crazy?' he hissed, in English, from between clenched white teeth.

As an opening gambit, she had heard better, but Molly didn't care. She had never seen anyone like this before—with his flashing black eyes and his perfect body and an air of strength and devil-may-careness that you simply didn't get with Englishmen.

'Sometimes.' She smiled at him, and cocked an eyebrow. 'Aren't you?' she said gravely. 'Crazy is good.'

He was expecting a tongue-tied and stumbling answer—not a cool retort in a voice as confident as his own.

There was a moment's pause—a heartbeat and a lifetime of a pause—before he began to laugh, and it sounded as delicious as the sprinkle of fresh water on sun-baked stone.

But then his eyes grew serious.

'You are not wearing helmets,' he growled. 'These roads are not like your English roads.'

'You can say that again,' murmured Molly. She thought of the fumes and the bad-tempered drivers back home, and compared them to Pondiki's clean and silent beauty.

He narrowed his eyes. 'You will both come with me,' he ordered abruptly. 'And you will wear helmets back.'

It was ironic that if anyone else had spoken to her

like that, then Molly would probably have refused, on principle. But now that she had found him, she didn't want to lose sight of him and, quite honestly, if he had told her that she was going to be put in handcuffs for the return journey, then she couldn't have seen herself uttering a word of objection.

He ordered coffee and they drank it on the terrace of his father's hotel, with its breathtaking views over the sea. Only Molly found it hard to concentrate on the view.

So did Dimitri. He shook himself slightly, as if trying to shake off the inexplicable spell she seemed to have cast over him.

Beautiful young women came to his island every summer and he was no innocent. Greek men lived very defined lives. Greek women were strictly out of bounds until marriage. If a man had trouble-free temptations of the flesh, then why not enjoy them while he could?

But this Molly was different, and he could not work out why. It was not just her pure, clean beauty, nor the sparkle of mischief which lit her ice-blue eyes. She had something which he wanted, something which made him ache unbearably.

He gave them helmets and saw them safely away, but just before Molly put hers on he lifted a hand to lightly brush a stray strand of hair away from her brow and their eyes met in a long, spine-tingling moment.

It felt like the most erotic thing which had ever happened to her, but then maybe it was—for what fumbled kisses could compare to the touch of a man like Dimitri?

'Can I take you for a drive some time?' he said, and felt her tremble.

She didn't hesitate. She wouldn't play games. Games were a waste of time when she only had six weeks on this island and she wasn't going to squander a single moment of them.

'Oh, yes, please,' she answered.

'Tomorrow?'

'Tomorrow,' she agreed.

And that was how it started.

She slept with him that very first day—she couldn't not have done—and afterwards she wept with sheer pleasure as he held her tightly, his expression fierce as he looked down at her, smoothing his palms over her damp skin, his eyes burning as brightly as lanterns.

'You were a virgin,' he stated, and his voice sounded strained.

'Not any more.' She touched her lips to his arm.

He closed his eyes, his feelings confused. He hadn't been expecting that, not from someone who looked like her. And he wondered if her virginity had been the indefinable something he had wanted. He had never slept with a virgin before, even though one day his wife would inevitably be one. And somehow it made it different. It shouldn't do, but it did. His kisses were tender on her eyelids and he pulled her closer against his bare skin.

'Sweet Molly,' he said softly.

'Sweet Dimitri,' she said drowsily.

She was slipping in deep and then deeper still, and maybe it showed because Elena tried to warn her. 'Molly, you know that Dimitri—'

'Yes, I know. Believe me, I know. He's Greek. I'm English.' She saw Elena's concerned face and smiled. 'I'm only here for the summer,' Molly said gently. 'Then I'm off to university. Don't worry, Elena—I'm not expecting to buy a white dress and have the people of Pondiki pin money onto it!'

Yet it was funny how you could know something on an intellectual level, but that didn't stop your foolish heart yearning for more. But she never showed it. Not to Dimitri, nor to Elena. She even tried to deny it to herself. And even though she sometimes wove little fantasies which involved her changing her university course to read Greek and returning here to help Dimitri run his hotel, she just tried to live each day for what it was. Paradise.

His parents, naturally enough, disliked her. She had never actually been introduced to them, but the couple of times she saw his mother at the weekday market in the square she was met with a stony-eyed look of hostility. But she understood that, too. They probably thought that she was some kind of loose-moralled tourist out for a summer of hot sex and there were enough of *those* on the island. She could hardly go up and explain that her son had captured her heart as well as her body, could she?

And there was a girl, too—a beautiful dark-eyed girl with a curtain of raven hair which fell to her slender waist. Molly saw her sometimes, and caught her looking at her with a sad, reproachful look.

'Who is that girl?' she asked Dimitri one afternoon.

He stared out to sea. 'Just a girl,' he said, and his voice sounded distant.

Something in his voice made her narrow her eyes, but she didn't ask another question; afterwards she suspected it was because she'd known what the answer would be.

Her time on Pondiki was slipping away like the soft white sand she trickled through her fingers, and, with only a couple of weeks until she had to return home, some American guys came to stay at the hotel.

One of them was gorgeous. Textbook perfect. James, with eyes as blue as her own and a lazy, outgoing manner. He liked her; he made that clear, and Molly thought how much simpler life would be if she liked him back.

But life was never that simple and she had eyes for only one man.

And then Dimitri rang, cancelling their date. It was her Sunday off and he had planned to take her climbing to the very top of Mount Urlin.

His voice sounded oddly strained. 'Molly, *agape mou*, I cannot make it. Not today.'

Molly bit her lip, trying not to feel disappointed, determined not to quiz him, but for once her resolution failed her.

'Oh, *why*, Dimitri?' she asked him plaintively. 'I've only got a couple more weeks and you've been promising to take me up there for ages!' Her voice softened. 'I've been so looking forward to it.'

And so had he. The summit of Mount Urlin was as stunning and as beautiful a spot as he had ever seen and he had planned to make love to her up there. The heat of desire warred briefly against the brick wall of duty. He sighed, then scowled at his reflection in the mirror. 'I know. And there will be another time—just not today. It's a family party.'

'Oh, I see.' And suddenly she did. Perfectly. Naturally, she would be excluded from anything which involved his family—his *real* life—for what did their time consist of other than deep, passionate kisses with their inevitable conclusion?

'Molly, I *have* to go.'

She said what was expected of her. 'Of course you do.'

She hung up, and then impulse sent her off to find Elena who was slicing up lemons in the bar. She looked up as Molly came in.

Molly poured herself a glass of fizzy water and perched on a high stool next to the counter. She twirled the lemon idly with her little finger and stared intently at the yellow circle bobbing around among the ice and the bubbles.

She glanced up. 'Dimitri's going to a family party tonight—do you know anything about it?'

Elena looked uncomfortable. 'Not really. It's just a party,' she said.

Molly would have needed to have been made of

stone not to have heard the evasion in her voice. 'At his home?' she questioned casually.

'At the hotel, I think.'

Molly bit her lip. She still had a night off. She still had use of the scooter. Why *shouldn't* she go and have a nose round, to find out what she could see? Because something wasn't right—she could feel it, deep down, and she could hear it too, in Elena's voice, see it in her reluctance to meet her eyes.

Her heart was pounding as she fetched her helmet and walked through the bar, where James was sitting, sipping from a glass of beer, wearing swimming trunks which were still damp from the sea. He crinkled his tanned face in an interested look as she stuffed her thick blonde hair up beneath the helmet.

'Off to see lover-boy?' he said ruefully.

Molly gave a forced smile. 'Not tonight. I just want to watch the sunset.'

'Like some company?'

She shook her head. 'No, thanks.'

'You take care, now—those roads are dangerous.'

'I will.'

But his words came back to haunt her. It wasn't just the roads which were dangerous—so were the emotions which drove her on to the bottom of the Urlin Road, towards Dimitri's hotel. She knew that what she was doing was wrong—like eavesdropping—yet she couldn't seem to stop herself.

She heard the sounds of a party well before she saw the twinkling of coloured lanterns, faint against the glorious sunset, and the mill of people clustering on the terrace. Laughter rang out over the water and Molly turned off her engine and parked the scooter in case someone heard her.

She felt like a jewel-thief as she silently approached the hotel, but she did not need to go far to recognise the two figures at the far end of the balcony, deep in conversation.

It was Dimitri and the beautiful raven-haired girl with the reproachful eyes. She saw the shadowy figure of his mother standing close by—with just the right amount of distance which spoke volumes of her role as chaperone.

Of course.

'Who is that girl?' Molly had asked him and he had replied, 'Just a girl.' And suddenly Molly understood. She was not ''just a girl''—she was Dimitri's girl. Oh, not now, maybe not even next week, or month, or even next year. But one day he would marry the beauty from Pondiki. He could have fun while he could, indeed—with whoever was there to provide it—but it certainly wouldn't be a Greek girl.

And maybe that was why she had felt the unspoken hostility—because, for once, the fun had become a little too serious. Dimitri liked her, she knew that— *really* liked her—he'd told her that and maybe his family had seen that, too. For once, it was not just some English girl who had been bedded and discarded after two nights.

Molly felt the taste of salt at the back of her throat as she willed the tears away. She had always known that there was a price to be paid for passion, and that she would break her heart when she left, but this changed everything and, instead, she felt the devastating and debilitating cocktail of anger and foolishness.

On autopilot she made her way back to her scooter and wheeled it a little way before starting it up, half fearing, half hoping that Dimitri would have somehow seen her, heard—and come after her to tell her that there was no other girl, no intended marriage and that she was the only one he wanted.

But life was not a fairy tale and Dimitri was a Greek pragmatist, not a romantic hero—even if he looked like one and acted like one most of the time.

By the time she got back she was shaking and James was still sitting in the bar, where she'd left him. He looked up when she walked in, and frowned.

'Looks like the sunset wasn't as good as you thought it would be,' he observed wryly. He indicated the chair. 'Have a drink?'

Molly hesitated for only a moment. She didn't want to be on her own, and what was the alternative to a drink with a kind, friendly face? Sit in her room and mope—worse, cry the unshed tears which were just dying to come out?

'I'd love one,' she said steadily.

'Ouzo?'

She shrugged, barely hearing him. 'Why not?'

She found the sickly-sweet taste of the aniseed drink vaguely comforting, and by the third her thoughts on the subject of Dimitri had become vehemently less charitable. But she kept them to herself. Better be a fool to yourself, than have the world know about it.

'Want to talk about it?' he asked.

'About what?'

'About what's made your eyes so sad?'

She shook her head with determination, but the movement made her feel slightly whoozy.

James narrowed his eyes. 'Have you eaten?'

She shook her head. 'Not hungry,' she mumbled.

'Say, Molly,' he said gently. 'Go easy on that stuff—it's dynamite.'

Maybe dynamite was just what she needed right now—something to blow away the crazy dreams she'd had about a man who had never promised anything more than a holiday romance.

'One for the road,' she said unsteadily, and waved her empty glass.

He looked uncertain, but he bought it for her. 'That's your last,' he warned.

'You can't stop me!' she said brightly.

But in the end he didn't need to. Molly went very hot and then very cold and her head began to swim.

'I don't feel so good,' she said indistinctly.

'You don't look so good,' he said. 'Maybe you need some food?'

Her face going very slightly green, Molly clapped her hand over her mouth.

James nodded. 'Food's out, then. Come on, Molly—you should go and sleep it off.'

Her legs felt like jelly and James had to put a restraining arm around her waist.

'For God's sake, Molly,' he said. 'Easy does it. Slow down, or everyone will think you're drunk.'

Molly gulped. 'Will you—will you see me up to my room please, James? I'm not sure my legs are going to carry me.'

A couple of dark heads swivelled in their direction as James led her out of the bar and up the narrow, rickety staircase at the back, but she barely noticed them. She stumbled into the room and collapsed on the narrow single bed, and shut her eyes.

'The room's going round and round,' she moaned.

'Open your eyes, then.'

'I *can't.*'

'Molly, turn onto your side,' he said urgently.

'Lemme sleep.'

'*No.*'

She felt sick and alone and frightened. Dimitri was somewhere else with the girl with raven hair and one day he would marry her. She stared up into the tanned face which kept shifting in and out of focus. 'Don't leave me, James.'

'I ain't going nowhere,' he said firmly. 'Here. You're hot.' He loosened two buttons on her sundress and her eyes flew open in alarm. His mouth twisted. 'Don't worry about a thing, Molly,' he said drily. 'I've never particularly been into women who are in love with someone else, and I've never had to stoop quite so low as to take advantage of someone who's drunk.'

She opened her mouth to deny the first part of his statement, but then shut it again, and a kind of stifled sob came out instead.

'It's okay,' soothed James as he fanned her with a magazine. 'You're going to be okay.'

And that was how Dimitri found them. Only by then it was later, much later—and James had fallen asleep on the bed beside her, still in his bathing trunks and a protective hand was possessively caught against her waist.

She discovered afterwards, from Elena, that someone had overheard her in the bar, asking James to take her upstairs, and had made it their responsibility to let Dimitri know. And soon after that he had burst into her room and she would never forget the expression on his face as her glued-up eyelids somehow opened. As if he couldn't believe it, and yet, oddly enough—as though he *wanted* to believe it.

And she didn't even have the opportunity to offer him an explanation, because he refused to see her again and she was too proud to beg—and, besides, Dimitri had his pride, too. The look of fury on his face told her that she had betrayed him, and in a way which meant that the rest of the island would know. And Pondiki was too small a place to tolerate such outrageous behaviour as a woman taking another man to her room, no matter what the reason.

'Why didn't you call for *me*?' Elena asked her sadly as Molly packed her clothes.

Molly shook her head. Didn't matter what she said. Not now.

'Is Dimitri going to marry Malantha?' she asked, her eyes clear and questioning. 'Tell me, honestly.'

Elena shrugged. 'Probably.' Her expression softened. 'That's the way things work, Molly.'

So that was that. Things would never be the same. They couldn't possibly be.

She left the following evening. Her employers understood without needing any explanation, which told Molly exactly how fast news travelled around Pondiki. And she had never felt quite so enveloped by a sense of shame—as though she had let everyone down, herself included—even though nothing had happened. But if she protested *that*, then who would believe her?

She looked around her in the tiny airport terminal—some last fairy-tale hope refusing to die as she imagined that he might suddenly run in, his dark eyes shining as he caught her into his strong arms, telling her that it had all been a terrible mistake. That he was liberated enough to understand her explanation.

But he didn't come.

Instead, she boarded the plane, and not until after the take-off—when the lights of Pondiki became as twinkingly distant as the stars above them—did she allow the first tears to slide from behind her tightly closed eyelids....

Molly blinked. The photo had become blurred and she realised to her surprise that there were tears in her eyes now. Quickly, she wiped them away and put the photo back in the box and snapped it shut.

There was nothing wrong with mourning the past, she decided, just so long as you weren't foolish enough to get it muddled up with the present.

If she could manage to have a civilised and friendly relationship with her ex-husband, then surely it wouldn't kill her to be polite to Dimitri for a few short weeks.

And, besides, he was coming to her party now. She really didn't have any choice in the matter.

CHAPTER FOUR

MOLLY drew in a deep breath as she surveyed the dazzle of gold which was reflected back from the mirror.

Was the dress too risqué?

The sales assistant had assured her not. 'For a party? Not at all! You have a wonderful figure, Madam,' she had purred. 'Why not show it off to advantage?'

Was that what she was doing? Was that why she had let herself be talked into buying it—fuelled by some belated desire to have Dimitri see what he had missed? That she was a different, grown-up Molly. A new person.

Because the old Molly would certainly never have worn a dress like *this*.

It was made of a dull, gleaming gold material and it fell in soft drapes to her knees and clung like melted butter to her body. At the back it was completely bare, leaving lots of skin on show, and she had rubbed moisturiser all over herself so that she gleamed as subtly as the dress.

She turned away from her reflection as the sound of the doorbell heralded the arrival of the first guests and she fixed a smile to her lips as she went into the hall to greet them.

But inside, she was on tenterhooks, starting every time the wretched doorbell rang and trying not to look disappointed when it was anyone—everyone— except Dimitri. She felt like a teenager again, with that horrible churned-up mixture of expectation and excitement and dread, and she felt angry with herself for wanting to see him so much. And angry with him for making her wait.

She had convinced herself that he had changed his mind and he wasn't coming after all, and telling herself that it was the best possible outcome for all concerned, when the doorbell sounded again, and she could see his tall, shadowy figure outlined through the stained glass.

Her heart began to speed erratically beneath her silk-covered breasts and her fingers were trembling as she opened the door and said, in a voice which didn't sound quite like her own, 'Dimitri! Hi! So glad you could make it—come in!' If it sounded rehearsed, then that was because it was—she had searched hard for just the right combination of casual greetings.

For a moment Dimitri didn't move, but that was because he didn't dare to. He scarcely recognised her—this shiny, beautiful, sexy blonde creature with her hair piled high up on her head. She looked a contradiction in terms—both so untouchable, and yet so eminently touchable.

He felt blood pounding at all his pulse-points. Temples. Wrists. Groin. His mouth twisted into an odd kind of smile.

'Molly,' he said unsteadily. 'You look...*oreos*.'

She knew the word beautiful from her time in Pondiki, but, even if she hadn't, she would have known that the word was a compliment. No, she amended silently. Compliment was the wrong word. When a man paid you a compliment, he shouldn't look as though the word were being torn reluctantly and sourly from his mouth, like a man having his teeth pulled. Nor should his eyes, black and hot and smouldering, rove over you in such a way that you felt desired and yet...resented.

'You might say it as though you meant it,' she commented breathlessly.

He raised his dark eyebrows in arrogant query, perversely angry at the sudden and overwhelming state of arousal in which he now found himself. He was a man used to dampening the hunger of the flesh when required, yet now his body was stubbornly refusing to obey his will.

'Surely you do not doubt that, *agape mou*?' he queried softly. 'Every man in the room will be wondering what—if anything—you are wearing beneath that outrageous gown.' Black eyes glittered an intense, hungry fire. 'And wondering if they will be lucky enough to be the one to remove it at the end of the evening.'

Molly's heart clenched as she imagined him doing just that, but she shook her head in an expression of amused outrage. 'I should ask you to leave for saying something like that!'

'But it is the truth. A dress like that is sending out

a very definite message.' He shrugged. 'I imagine that is why you wore it.'

What could she say? That she had wanted to look her most impressive best? And that his mocking assessment made her wish that she had covered herself up from head to toe?

She pulled herself together. 'Are you going to stand here all night insulting me, or would you like a drink?'

He allowed himself the brief and frustrating fantasy of refusing. Of pulling her outside, instead. Of taking her into his arms and kissing her until she was in such a fevered state of need that she would ignore all her party guests and take him upstairs and spend the rest of the night letting him make love to her.

And wondered why he had consented to endure a noisy party filled with people who would no doubt be vying for her attention all night.

But this was called playing the game and he could not have her. Not here and not now and not yet. His eyes gleamed. 'A drink would be wonderful.'

She pointed with a finger which was not quite steady, though her voice thankfully was. 'Everyone's in here.'

Molly was aware of the momentary lull in the buzz of party chatter as they walked into the main reception room. She grabbed a glass from a circulating waiter and handed it to him. 'Champagne okay?'

'Champagne is always perfect.' He took the flute and studied the fizzing bubbles for a moment, then raised his head and lifted his glass to her, his eyes never leaving her face as he took a sip of champagne, and Molly thought that if any other man had done that she would have found it unspeakably corny. Yet when Dimitri did it…she found herself gazing back, tempted to lose herself in the black blaze from his eyes.

She smiled instead. 'You must let me introduce you to some people who will be dying to meet you.'

She thought that there would certainly be no shortage of takers. He put every other man in the shade—quite literally—with his towering height and the hard-packed muscular body. Dark, tailored trousers and a white silk shirt of breathtaking simplicity showed off his muscular physique to perfection and, judging by the covert glances cast in their direction, Molly wasn't the only woman in the room who thought so.

His rugged face was darkened by the hint of five o'clock shadow and yet she suspected that it couldn't have been too long since he had shaved. And maybe women just homed in automatically on that, the way they had been programmed to do—the shadowed jaw sending out the subliminal signal that here was a man at his most glorious and virile peak.

Her palms felt clammy and surreptitiously she smoothed them down over her shiny gold hips. 'Now, let me see—who would you like to meet?' But it was an academic question—she didn't even have to go in search of someone, because a stunning redhead had appeared, her question directed at Molly, but her attention fixed on Dimitri.

'Hello! Just who is *this*, Molly?' she demanded, with a delighted little smile. 'And where have you been hiding him away?'

Molly smiled. 'Hello, Alison,' she said, slightly amused by her friend's reaction. No prizes for subtlety *there*—she was eyeing him with unashamed interest—though maybe Dimitri liked that. She stole a glance at him. Difficult to tell, with that dark, shadowed face giving nothing away. It never had—even when he had been making love to her, his eyes had been shuttered, his thoughts a complete mystery. 'This is Dimitri Nicharos. Dimitri—I'd like you to meet Alison Dempster.'

'Hello, Alison,' he said softly, and smiled, and Molly saw Alison almost dissolve beneath the sensual impact of that voice, that face, that body, that smile.

'You're Greek?' enquired Alison breathlessly.

'Indeed I am. But as you will see, I come bearing no gifts—so there is no need for you to beware!'

'Are you sure?' laughed Alison.

Dimitri looked at Molly, thinking how edgy she looked. 'How do you two know each other?'

'Oh, I've known Alison and Will for years,' Molly answered. 'He's over there.' She pointed at an owlish lawyer who stood laughing with a small group of men.

Alison raised her eyebrows in surprise, as if to say, Why the hell did you have to tell him *that*? And Molly wondered herself. She knew that married women liked to flirt at parties—it was all part of the sophisticated urbane game of life they played. So was it a ploy to tell Dimitri that Alison was definitely not available—even though she had no right to be possessive about him?

Dimitri sipped his champagne. What a mine field of emotions a party always threw up! He was beginning to enjoy himself. 'You've known each other for a long time?'

It was clearly Alison's turn to get her own back.

'We met through Molly's ex-husband,' she said chattily. 'He came to my husband for advice, when he was setting up his business.' She turned a pair of innocent green eyes up to him. 'Have you met Hugo yet?'

'Unfortunately, no.' Black eyes glittered in Molly's direction. 'Not yet.'

Molly was beginning to wish that she were anywhere other than here, but there was a whole evening to get through, and she was the hostess. And she was not going to spend it keeping tabs on *him*. 'Can I get you another drink, Dimitri?'

He shook his head. 'I'm fine. Go and see to your guests—don't feel you have to look after me.'

She felt her cheeks burn, feeling like an unwelcome fly which had just been swatted away. Saw Alison's curious glance. 'Right. Well, I'll leave you to it,' she said, rather weakly.

She moved away to flit between groups of people, introducing those who didn't know each other and drawing in would-be outsiders with a skill she had learned through years of attending corporate events with Hugo.

Waitresses offered plates of expensive delicacies which satisfied the taste buds but not the appetite, but Molly hadn't wanted the fuss of a full meal. They refilled glasses as music played softly in the background and people began to relax and let their guard down.

To an outsider, it must have seemed like a good party—but to Molly it was an endurance test from beginning to end. Because it was as if no one else in the room existed, save him. He dominated his surroundings, simply by being. She still wanted him, she realised.

She let her gaze drift across to him. He was surrounded by a small group of men, and he was making them laugh and that somehow surprised her. Had she thought that he would be commandeered by women all evening? And yet he was mixing like a seasoned party expert, fitting easily into her circle of friends. He seemed as cosmopolitan and sophisticated as the rest of them, and she wondered whether he socialised much on Pondiki.

She glanced across the room and he looked up, his black eyes glittering, as if he had sensed that she was watching him and she quickly turned away, half afraid that he might be able to guess at her thoughts.

But Alison had seen her and came to stand next to her.

'We're about to leave. Will has got a big case in the morning,' she said. 'Thanks for a lovely party.'

Molly smiled. 'My pleasure.'

There was a moment's silence. 'He's quite something,' Alison remarked.

'Who?'

'The man in the moon, of course!' Alison giggled. '*Who!* Molly, I'm one of your oldest friends, you can't fool me—the Gorgeous Greek, of course. Who is he?'

'Someone I knew years ago.'

'And he's back in your life?'

Molly shook her head. 'Oh, no, he's just…passing through.'

'Well, I've never seen someone exert so much magnetism over women. Myself included,' Alison added ruefully. 'There isn't a woman in the room who hasn't been eyeing him like a hungry tiger all night!'

Molly's shoulders felt bare and exposed in the flirty golden gown and her skin suddenly felt chilled. She knew what Alison meant. Despite his air of sophistication and the immaculate clothes he wore, nothing could disguise the fact that Dimitri was the kind of man which cities did not breed. There wasn't another man in the room who looked as though he could catch a fish with his bare hands, or climb a tree as effortlessly as she had seen him do. 'That's because he likes women—but then, Greek men do and women home in on that.'

'Aren't you in danger of being a touch stereotypical?'

'Not really, no. They're different from English

men.' Molly successfully suppressed an erotic shiver of memory. So different.

'How?' Alison's face was interested.

'Oh, they think about women differently, treat them differently. A woman was put on this earth to love,' she recited from memory, without even realising that she was doing so. 'Women are soft but men are hard and the two complement each other.' Her cheeks went pink as she recognised just how much she had given away.

'So he was your lover?' guessed Alison slowly.

'I'm surprised it took you so long to ask.'

'I'm surprised you didn't tell me.'

Had she really hoped that by inviting him she would be able to keep it secret? Molly supposed that it was inevitable that Alison might have guessed—even if she hadn't given her such glaring great signposts along the way. She nodded. 'Yes. He was. A long time ago.'

'And he hurt you?'

'Oh, you know—it was just the normal teenage heartbreak. A youthful affair that ended naturally, that's all.' It was nothing but the truth—but it was funny how bare and inadequate the truth could sometimes sound.

There was silence for a moment. 'But you still want him?'

Molly shook her head. 'Not any more. I'm not interested in him. Not now.'

'I think you are,' contradicted Alison. 'You may not want to be, but you are—it's written all over you.

You might as well have a huge sign stuck to your forehead, saying "Make love to me, Dimitri!"'

Molly's eyes widened. 'Oh, God,' she breathed. 'Is it that obvious?'

'Maybe only to me—but that's because I know you.' She smiled. 'There's no need to look so tragic, Molly! Lots of women want men they know are trouble—I'm afraid that some of the qualities which make them trouble are the same qualities which make them irresistible. But you don't have to submit to him, you know! Oh-oh, he's coming over! I'll be a good friend—time I was going, I think.'

Molly looked after Alison helplessly as she began to weave her way through the room in search of her husband. Part of her wanted to say, *Don't go! Please don't leave me with this man who exudes the kind of danger and excitement I can do without!* But then Dimitri was there, towering beside her, the raw male scent of him so evocatively familiar, and all she could think was, *He's here—he's here at last—and I have him all to myself!*

Dimitri looked down at her and saw the brief tremble of her lips. Her gold-covered breasts rose and fell as she breathed, and not for the first time desire and frustration combined to make him wonder just for whose benefit she had worn such an outrageously sexy garment. A tight, hot fist of predatory jealousy hit him somewhere in the solar plexus. 'This is quite some party, Molly,' he observed coolly.

'You sound surprised.'

'Do I? I suppose I am a little.' He fixed her with a steady black stare. 'So who pays for it?'

She stared back, aware of the undercurrent of hostility. 'I'm not quite sure I understand what you mean.'

'Don't you?' He looked around the room. 'You live in a big house. You serve champagne to your guests. So either your travel books earn you a huge income, or your divorce settlement was exceptionally generous. Or...' He paused deliberately.

'Or what?'

He shrugged. 'Maybe you have a lover who likes to lavish things on you.' He glanced around the room. 'Someone here tonight, perhaps—a secret lover?'

'A kept woman, you mean?' she demanded. 'Somebody's mistress? One of my friend's husbands, perhaps?'

'Why not?'

'You really think that's the way I live my life?'

'How should I know, *agape mou*? Women do.'

'Not this woman,' she said furiously. 'If you must know, then, yes, my writing pays enough to support me. I'm lucky enough not to have a mortgage because, yes, my divorce settlement *was* generous—but it was nothing more than fair, since I helped my husband set up and run his business! Does that answer your insulting question, Dimitri?'

He allowed himself the slow expulsion of a breath he had not even realised he was holding. So there wasn't someone. He looked down into her furious face, where the cat-shaped eyes sparked blue fire at him, and he smiled, wishing that they were alone and that he could subdue her temper with a kiss. 'Then I must congratulate you on your independence.'

Molly's furious expression didn't waver. 'Is that all you've got to say?'

'Why are you so offended, Molly?' he mused. 'It's the way of the world. Rich men support beautiful women—it's been going on since the beginning of time. Simply a trade of commodities, that's all.'

He was unbelievable! He hadn't even had the grace to apologise! Well, she was not going to have a stand-up fight with him in front of her friends. 'I'd better go and see my guests out,' she said icily. 'If you want to leave, then please don't let me keep you, Dimitri.'

But he didn't bite. Instead, he wandered across the room and began talking to Molly's accountant, much to her annoyance. And then, just when she was wondering whether he was intending to be the last to leave, and her heart had begun to thunder at the prospect of *that*, he came to say goodbye.

'Thank you for coming,' she said stiffly. But her anger seemed to have fled, dissolved by the potent power of his proximity and stupidly, illogically—she wanted him to stay.

'Thank you for having me,' he said softly. 'It was a good party.'

That wasn't what it felt like to her. She closed the door behind him, and briefly laid her hot forehead on a cool pane of glass, feeling weary and deflated. Well, she had done her neighbourly duty. With a little bit of planning and foresight, their paths need never cross again.

CHAPTER FIVE

MOLLY woke the next morning with a splitting head-ache, which she thought was slightly unfair as she had drunk nothing more than a couple of glasses of champagne. Maybe it had more to do with an unsettled night, and dreams invaded by a man she had never thought she would see again.

She showered and dressed, tied her hair back and went downstairs, preparing herself for the aftermath of the party, and it was as bad as she had thought. True, her friends were well behaved and fairly grown up in their outlook—there were no cigarettes stubbed out on the rugs, nor spillages of wine or beer over the furniture. But she still found a number of half-full glasses concealed behind the curtains and there were stacks of glasses to unload from the dishwasher before the next lot could be put in.

She ate a bowl of cherries and set to work, mopping the kitchen floor and wiping down all the surfaces and throwing all the leftover bits of party food into the bin. The place was just starting to look like home again when the doorbell rang and she went to answer it, her footsteps slowing as her heart-rate soared when she saw it was Dimitri.

She could always ignore his summons, of course.

Deliberately not answer the door and then he might get the message.

But what message would that be? That she didn't want to see him? Because then the message would be a lie. Or, at least, a very mixed-up message— nearly as mixed-up as she felt inside. She *did* want to see him, that was the trouble.

She opened the door. 'What do you want?' she asked, but the words faded away into nothing when she saw that he was carrying an enormous bunch of pink and yellow roses, big as fists. The clashing colours shouldn't have worked, but somehow they did; they looked wild and exotic—and so did he. 'For me?' she said stupidly as he held them out to her.

'Who else?' He thought how much more beautiful she looked this morning, with her pale, bare face and the faint blue smudges beneath her eyes. Last night, the too-glamourous gown had made her look like someone out of a magazine. Unreal and unknown. This Molly looked like a living and breathing woman and he wanted to touch her.

'Oh, they're gorgeous! You didn't have to do that,' she said instinctively, burying her nose in their petals, partly to inhale the glorious scent but partly because her cheeks had flushed pink with pleasure and inwardly she cursed herself. Acting as if she had never received a bouquet before!

'Yes, I did,' he contradicted softly. 'You very sweetly invited me into your home and I did nothing but insult you.'

She looked up then. 'Yes, you did,' she agreed.

'All that ridiculous stuff about me being a kept woman! As if!'

He bit back a smile. She had answered him back the very first time he had met her, and she was still doing it. 'So do you forgive me, Molly?'

She looked into the face she knew so well, and yet scarcely knew at all, and knew that she was in danger of forgiving him almost anything. 'Only if you promise never to make any assumptions about me again. And that includes your assumption that I was intimate with James. I was not. Understand?'

Reluctantly, he nodded. '*Ne*, Molly,' he sighed. 'I understand.' The black eyes gleamed. 'Now are you going to invite me in?'

'Is that why you bought me the flowers?'

'The flowers were to say sorry.'

'But coffee would be a bonus, right?'

'Coffee would be a good start,' he agreed steadily.

But a start to what? There was a split-second where logic warred with the heady danger of the unknown, but the soft gleam from his eyes made logic fall by the wayside. 'I won't have time to sit down and chat,' she warned as she opened the door wider. 'I'm clearing up after the party.'

'Then let me help.'

'You!' Molly couldn't resist it. 'Doing ''women's'' work?' She raised her eyebrows at him challengingly. 'Whatever next?'

'Do you mend your own car?'

'I send it to the garage.'

'Where, no doubt, the place is overrun by female mechanics?'

She opened her mouth and shut it again. 'None you'd notice.' Molly sighed. 'Okay, you win.'

But there was no victory for Dimitri. Not yet. He knew the prize he wanted, but he must tread carefully, for Molly was no longer an eighteen-year-old lulled and seduced by the hot beat of the sun and the power of her sexual awakening.

The kitchen was bathed in sunlight, and as she walked into it, her arms full of the fragrant flowers, Molly thought that she had never really seen it before. The scent of coffee which wafted from the pot smelt so *intensely* of coffee, just as the newly washed glasses gleamed brighter than diamonds. Outside she could hear the birds chirruping in the garden and they had never seemed to sing so loud as they did then. Her senses were raw, she realised, and he was the cause of it, and yet the sensations were too persuasive for her to want to do anything to stop him. And she wasn't doing anything wrong, was she? She was only making him a cup of coffee, for heaven's sake.

'I'd better put these in water,' she said, and even her voice sounded different, low and clear, like a bell.

He watched in silence as she pulled a huge vase from beneath the sink and turned the tap on full, so that it splashed all over her, and slopped over the sides of the vase.

'You're making a mess,' he observed softly.

'Yes.'

She didn't look round. She could feel her neck growing warm and contrasting with the splash which had plastered her little vest-top to her breasts like an icy skin. And suddenly she didn't know what to do, afraid to move or to say anything for fear that he would read the terrible hunger in her eyes. Her fingers were trembling as she began to spear the roses into the vase. She could hear him moving behind her, could feel his body heat, though he wasn't touching her.

'So what are we going to do about it?'

'What?' she questioned weakly, for his breath was warm against her neck.

'This.' His hand moved round to cup her soaking breast, and he closed his eyes as he felt it peak against the palm of his hand. 'You're so wet,' he murmured.

Her knees sagged, and she gripped the forgotten flower, hard. 'Ow!'

He turned her round. 'What have you done?'

She was staring at her hand, hazily aware of the scarlet contrast of blood against her pale skin. 'Pricked myself. On the thorn.'

'Let me see.'

She lifted her eyes to his as he took her hand and studied the injured finger. And then, very deliberately, he raised it to his mouth and began to suck on the blood, his eyes never leaving her face, and it felt almost indecently erotic.

'Dimitri,' she whispered.

'*Ne?*' His voice sounded muffled against her skin.

'Stop it.'

'The bleeding? That is what I am trying to do, *agape mou.*'

He was wilfully misunderstanding her, but she didn't care. It felt like heaven to have him touch her again—the aching familiarity mixed with the delight of the new and unknown. And yet she despaired. One touch and she was jelly. Marshmallow. Everything that was soft and sweet and subtly overpowering. And hadn't it always been like this?

He took the finger from his mouth and leaned forward and kissed her instead. She could taste the saltiness of her blood on his lips and she closed her eyes, swayed, gripped his shoulders, pressing her fingers hard into the silken sinews of his flesh, feeling him shudder and glad of it, sensing a barely restrained abandon which matched her own.

He took his mouth away from hers and looked down at her, his eyes black and glittering with both danger and promise. 'Take this off,' he ordered, his fingers inching beneath the soaking vest-top to feel the cool skin beneath.

But Molly was about as much use as a statue, frozen to the spot with desire, and he gave a little click, and then a slow smile as he shook his head in mock reprimand.

'It seems like I will have to do it myself,' he murmured. He peeled the top over her head and tossed it with arrogant disregard onto the floor and then he stared down at her lace-covered breasts, as if he had just unwrapped the most delicious present. And some of his habitual control slipped away. 'Oh, Molly,' he moaned softly. 'Molly.'

She knew that his groaned delight was for her breasts, and the prospect of what was to come and she wished it was more than that—of course she did. She wanted to know that the pleasure was because it was *her*, and her and only her. But that was a woman thing—wanting more than a man was prepared to offer.

'Oh, God!' Her head jerked back as his lips began to tease the tip of her breast through the bra, so that the lace felt like barbed wire on the sensitised flesh. She gripped his dark head between her hands as he opened his mouth and began to suckle her. 'Dimitri, don't!'

He ignored her, drifting his hand down over the flat of her stomach, snapping open the poppers of the little denim skirt she wore, so that it fell uselessly to her feet. Had she worn the tiny little garment knowing the ease with which it could be removed? he wondered. His finger skimmed aside the tiny panel of her panties and slid into the honeyed slickness of her flesh. Did she always make herself so delightfully accessible?

Again, the hot shaft of jealousy shot through him, fuelling a hunger which was already near-combustible and he moved his hand away, heard her squeaked protest, and lifted her up into his arms instead.

Dazedly, she looked up at him. It was like something out of a dream and yet nothing could be more real than the way she felt. Every nerve ending felt sizzling, sensitised, clamouring for him.

'What are you doing?'

The strain of trying to think straight made his voice harden. 'What do you think I'm doing?' he ground out. 'You want that I should take you here, in the kitchen, among the roses and the pots and pans?'

Any minute now and she was going to explode. 'Just take me somewhere; anywhere,' she begged. 'Upstairs.'

Despite the heated flames of his building desire, there remained in him a coolly questioning part which wondered if the journey upstairs would give her time to change her mind. But then he noted the rosy flush which outlined her high cheekbones, the fevered glittering of her eyes and he knew that she was as hell-bent on this as he was.

And her eagerness disconcerted him almost as much as it satisfied him. For equal desire meant that there would be no mastery. If her longing matched his, then they were going to be on an equal playing field. And he was a man who usually delighted in a sense of mastery.

He thought of going upstairs. To the bedroom she had shared with her husband? Or perhaps to the spare room, where she usually took her lovers? A shiver of distaste ran through him.

He shook his head, and he dipped his head, kissed her lips and felt her tremble. 'No. Not upstairs.'

'W-where?' she questioned dazedly, as if it were his house and not hers.

He carried her from the kitchen, straight into the sitting room and she looked around her. 'Dimitri?' she questioned, in a kind of befuddled daze, but by then he had reached the huge sofa, and had put her down and was turning to draw the heavy velvet curtains so that the room was dimmed with the surreal glow of blocked-out daylight. 'H-here?'

He turned back and began to walk towards her, kicking off his shoes and unbuttoning his shirt as he did so. 'Why not?' He saw her eyes widen as the shirt fluttered to the ground like a white flag of surrender, and the irony of that did not escape him. For hadn't he once told himself that, if she were the last woman on earth, he would not make love to her again? No matter if she fell to her knees before him and begged him to. But he had been young then, hotheaded and impetuous. He unzipped his trousers and stepped out of them and it satisfied his male ego to hear her gasp when she saw just how aroused he was.

But he honestly could not remember ever feeling as aroused as this. As if it were the first time and the last time and all the times in between.

He saw her bite her lip as he moved over her. He shifted away from her a fraction. 'Molly?'

She shook her head. It would be sheer folly and weakness to say that the sight of his body was unbearably poignant—for what conclusion would he draw from that? That there had been no other to compare with him? And there hadn't been, had there? Never.

She wrapped her arms tightly around his naked back and kissed him back, and there was something so evocative about that kiss that she had to will back a little sob.

He moved his lips to her neck, her breasts, and it felt like drowning in slick, sweet and honeyed waters from which there could be no escape—but who was trying? Not Molly. It had been too long. Much, much too long. She felt as though her body had been as dry and as arid as a desert, and Dimitri's lips were bringing her flooding back to life, her blood beating out a remorseless, drenching heat in her veins once more.

'Dimitri,' she breathed, and her hands came up to lock themselves around his head, imprisoning *him*, just in case *he* dared try to escape.

'I'm here,' he groaned, though he felt as if he had shifted onto another planet.

Oh, God, she wanted him so badly—but was she just asking for trouble and heartbreak? Resurrecting something which had hurt her so much. And hadn't the pain healed now? By letting him make love to her again, wasn't she in danger of reopening the wound and making it raw and livid all over again?

She pulled her lips away from his. 'I feel that I ought to stop you,' she said indistinctly.

'But you will not stop me.'

No. She could not. Not now. Not when he was sliding her panties down over her knees like that.

'Oh, God! Dimitri!'

'You like that?'

'Oh!' His fingertips were playing with her heated flesh, like a virtuoso playing some exquisite solo on the violin. Oh, sweet heaven—she would *die* if he made her wait much longer.

She writhed hard against him and heard him utter a curse, and she let her eyelids flutter open to see the dark helplessness on his face.

'What are you trying to do to me, *agape mou*?' he demanded, in a voice of dangerous silk which made her pulses race even faster.

She writhed again, driven by instinct and desire, unable to stop herself. 'What do you think I'm trying to do, Dimitri?' she murmured distractedly.

He caught a rope of her silken hair in his hand and possessively wound it round his fingers, drawing her face closer to his. 'I cannot believe that you know so little of men not to realise that if you continue to do that, then this will all be over very quickly.'

The inference was clear—that she had an encyclopaedic knowledge of the opposite sex, but at that moment his fingers untangled themselves from her hair and he reached out to trace the outline of her lips with a fingertip touch which was so gentle that it disarmed.

'Take it slowly, *ne*?'

'I don't know that I can,' she said, a slight note of desperation touching her voice.

He tilted her chin with his finger, frowned as he looked into her face and felt the tremble of excitement in her body. 'You want me very much, Molly,' he observed, a note of surprise in his voice.

She heard the disapproval, too. Did he think she was like this with other men? Doubt shivered over her once more, but then he had begun to kiss her—soft, searching kisses which became harder, more frantic, seeking kisses with a power to dissolve every last lingering inhibition. She had this, and she was going to savour every moment of it.

'Make love to me, Dimitri,' she urged. 'Now. Please.'

He entered her with one slow, powerful thrust, impaling her, making her his and she felt it pierce her almost to her heart as he began to move inside her, almost passing out with pleasure as he began a slow rhythm, touching his lips to hers as he did so. It seemed so familiar and yet so poignantly different—and, oh, how could she have forgotten just how wonderful it felt, to be made love to by a man?

This man.

She wrapped her legs possessively around his back and heard him groan in response.

He lost himself in her dark, warm heat—giving himself up to sensation, but not completely—watching Molly, revelling in her own uninhibited pleasure, nearly going out of his mind as she moved in perfect synchrony with him. Her eyes were closed and her lips were parted. And only when did she gasp, once, his name, and her eyes snap open in a kind of startled recognition—did he allow himself to let go, and it went on and on and on. Unknown words were wrenched from his mouth as the sound of her small, gasping cries rang in his ears.

There was a time—how long, she couldn't have said—when they just lay there, gathering their breath, half-shuddering bodies still joined and slick with sweat, his head bent upon her shoulder, his lips pressed against her skin.

Molly stared at the ceiling. Now what?

Fighting sleep, she stirred a little beneath the weight of his inert body and realised that he had fallen asleep. She shook him, gently, her fingertips kneading into the oiled silk of his skin. 'Dimitri.'

From the depths of some heavenly dream, Dimitri made a little moan of protest. From some dreams you never wanted to waken.

'Dimitri!'

He felt himself stir inside her sweet, wet warmth. He was still asleep! He moved his body luxuriously against the soft, giving flesh which enfolded his.

'Will you wake up?'

Okay, he was awake, but the reality was even better than the dream. He smiled against her neck, realising that he was still inside her, and he began to grow hard once more, instinctively beginning to move.

She fought desire. Fought her greedy wish to have him do it to her one more time, but, oh, it wasn't easy. 'Dimitri!' she said, as sternly as an irate schoolmistress.

His eyes opened, taking in his surroundings with

a sense of disbelief. Here. On Molly's sofa. In Molly's sitting room. In Molly.

He groaned as he withdrew, and looked down at her face, all rosy and glowing, the icy-blue eyes slitted by lids which were heavy and drowsy.

She met his impassive gaze and in that moment she felt a million miles away from him—but then, she had to face it, she was. Just because they still had that whatever-it-was which made them dynamite together sexually—well, it was nothing more than that. Chemistry. Attraction—call it what you wanted.

'Molly,' he said softly.

She was not going to be an emotional limpet. She was going to think like a man, even if inside she felt as vulnerable as any woman. 'Mmm?'

'That was…amazing.'

A tinge of hysteria nearly surfaced. She felt like asking him for marks out of ten, but she didn't, just kept the dreamy smile of fulfilment pinned to her lips, which wasn't exactly difficult. 'Yes, it was,' she agreed calmly.

He levered himself up onto one elbow, and idly lifted a stray strand of damp hair from her forehead and that one gesture almost broke her resolve. For that was how it had started, wasn't it? All those years ago. The same thoughtful, almost gentle action which seemed so at odds with the strong, powerful Greek with the ruggedly handsome face.

'So now what do we do?' he questioned.

'You mean, as of—right now?'

That had not been what he had meant, at all, and

she knew it. Left to him there was only one thing he would like to have done after making love to her and that was to make love to her all over again.

But he had to be sure of what Molly wanted or expected—and she had to know what his own agenda was. If she was one of those women who had started thinking hearts and flowers and happy-ever-after just because he had given her a spectacular orgasm, then this would—unfortunately—be the first and last time, however difficult he might find it.

Usually, his demands were met because he stated them openly and honestly, but this was going to be more difficult. In truth, it felt different from usual, but maybe that was because they had history between them. Molly had known him at the height of passionate and impressionable youth. He had told her things he had never told another woman, not even his wife—and Molly had to be certain in her mind that the man who had said those things no longer existed. How could he, after everything that had happened? Time took from you, as well as giving—and his idealistic dreams had long ago given way to the constraints of life in an adult world.

He bent his head to kiss the tip of her nose and saw her quickly shut her eyes.

'Molly?'

She opened them only when she had had time to compose herself. Whatever he said next she would deal with. She had no choice. She rubbed the tip of her finger along the outline of his mouth. 'What?'

'Shall we be lovers?'

Her heart lurched beneath her breast. 'I thought we just had.'

'I mean again.'

She knew that it would be uncool to ask for a timescale, but she needed to get things straight in her mind. 'You mean while you're in England?'

Dimitri narrowed his eyes. 'But of course.'

Well, that told her one thing—he certainly wasn't thinking long-term. He was here for weeks, no longer. The only question was whether she wanted to be his lover, although it was a pretty academic question. Of *course* she wanted to be his lover, but could she do it and survive with her heart intact?

She gave him a considering stare. 'You're saying that you want an affair?'

'Why not?'

She could think of plenty of reasons, but none that a man would understand, and especially a man like Dimitri. 'With no strings?' she asked.

His eyes narrowed in a swift look of surprise. 'That is supposed to be *my* line, Molly,' he murmured.

She knew it was, but she had deliberately taken the initiative away from him. If she let him lay down all the guidelines that would give him a position of power and she was only going to allow this to happen if power were shared. As equals.

'That's not an answer,' she pointed out.

He gave a soft, low laugh. 'Strings are the very last thing I want, or need. I am here for a little over a month—no more and no less. After that, I return to Pondiki.'

With his appetite presumably satisfied, and with her left feeling…what? Regret?

But wasn't life too short for that? After all, she was a mature woman now, and she was divorced. Maybe an affair with Dimitri was perfect for her at this stage in her life. Wasn't that the kind of decision that grown-up women made?

She wasn't looking for love—and if she was, she certainly wouldn't go looking for it with *him*. Neither did she want commitment—a man living with her, a one-on-one relationship with all the heavy demands that brought with it. She had already tried that and it hadn't worked.

And, yes, he had reacted badly all those years ago. He had accused her of things she had not done, even though he hadn't bothered to tell her that he was intended to another woman, but that should not have surprised her either. Because the man she had fallen for was precisely the kind of man who would be insanely jealous, who would live life on *his* terms without considering whether she should also live by those terms. He was, at heart, rather old-fashioned and that was part of his charm. It was not, she realised now, what she would want for a partner if she were looking for a partner—which she *wasn't*. But that didn't disqualify him from having the perfect qualities for a lover, did it?

'What about Zoe?' she asked.

His face grew shuttered. 'What about her?'

'Won't she mind?'

'She won't know, Molly.' There was a silence. 'This is just between you and me.'

Well, what had she expected? That he take her next door by the hand and introduce her to his daughter as his latest girlfriend? Giving their 'no strings' affair a veneer of respectability. 'So you're talking about a secret, clandestine affair?'

'There is no point in Zoe meeting you, surely you can understand that?'

'Oh, perfectly.'

He could hear the tremble of hurt in her voice. 'Look, I know it isn't ideal—'

'No, it isn't ideal!' she agreed, wondering if her objections would be enough to scare the hell out of him, to make him go away and find someone less demanding. And perhaps that would be best for them all—certainly for *her*. 'Dimitri—'

He shushed her by putting his finger on her lips and she answered by nibbling at it. He winced, but the slight discomfort turned him on. Unbearably. He remembered the scratch-marks she had once left on his back because, she'd told him, he had treated her like a second-class citizen in front of his friends. Maybe he had done, maybe he had been showing off—unwilling for his friends to see the macho Dimitri Nicharos doing the bidding of the blue-eyed Englishwoman who, by rights, should not have lasted beyond a few days. He had had to cover up with a T-shirt for a whole week and he had accused her of branding him and she had smiled a witchy kind of smile and kissed the weals she had made.

'Molly,' he soothed.

'You think I want to be hidden away, as if I'm something to be ashamed of!' She very nearly said that at least on Pondiki he had been open about it. But wasn't that because back then he'd had no responsibilities? But he had, a cynical voice in her head reminded her. He had had Malantha waiting patiently in the wings. Who knew what was going on in his current life—with all its secrets and its different compartments? 'Maybe you should find someone else.'

'But I don't want anyone else,' he said patiently. 'You are all the lover that any man could want, *agape*.'

'I sense there's a "but" coming.'

He nodded. 'But I have a daughter.'

'And you usually keep your lovers secret from her, do you?'

He shook his head. 'Usually there is no need because usually I travel solo,' he said. 'This is the first time that Zoe has been abroad with me.'

Molly was silent for a minute. Even his honesty about his 'usual' lovers hurt, when it had no right to hurt. What had she expected him to say? That she was the first lover he had taken since his wife had died? And wasn't that what she would have liked, deep down? She was doing exactly what she had vowed not to—giving him a hard time. Making demands that could not be met. Entertaining hopes which would not be met. Either she took what was on offer, or she turned her back on the proposal without another thought.

'I am a good lover, Molly,' he murmured.

'Oh, the arrogance, Dimitri! The conceit!' she mocked back. And the total lack of comprehension that women didn't choose lovers because they were dynamite in bed. Women chose men with their hearts, not their bodies—that was the difference between the sexes and that was where the danger lay.

But the flip side to danger was excitement, and excitement was what Dimitri was offering her. Yes, there was a risk that she would be hurt again, but what was life without risk? A life lived safely to safeguard against possible hurt was surely no life at all.

His thumb began to stroke at the cool flesh of her inner thigh and Molly felt herself squirm.

'That isn't fair,' she said weakly, feeling him stir in response, hard and pushed against the soft cushion of her belly.

'What isn't?'

She licked the finger that she had bitten. 'Using depraved methods to get me to agree to what you want.'

'Depraved? You think *that* is depraved? Molly, you haven't seen anything yet.' With a smooth movement, he pulled her to lie on top of him and entered her when she wasn't expecting it, and she sucked in an instinctive breath of protested pleasure.

'Dimitri!'

He began to move. 'Mmm?'

'I haven't given you my answer yet.'

He moved again, and he was taken aback by how good it felt, as good as before. No. He groaned. Better. Much better. With an effort, he opened his eyes, looking up at her to see her caught up in the rapture herself, her neck and breasts still rose-smudged from the time before. 'Then what is your answer to be, Molly?'

She touched his eyelids with her fingertip. Then his nose and his lips, as if rediscovering his beautiful face, even while their bodies were joined so intimately, and she was filled with warmth and an unbearable longing. 'It's yes,' she choked. 'You know it's yes!'

For how could it ever be anything else?

CHAPTER SIX

'WHAT time is it, *agape mou*?'

Molly peered over at the clock on the bedside table. 'Nearly twelve,' she yawned.

They were lying in bed. The sun was streaming in through the cracks in the blinds, which meant that they had precisely an hour before Dimitri would shower and dress and arrive home in time for Zoe to return. His arrivals and departures were like clockwork—and even the intervening hours had developed a pattern. They made love. She made coffee. They talked and then they made love again.

And then one of them would notice the time and Dimitri would sigh and shrug, and she would pretend not to care as he sauntered naked across the bedroom into the shower.

Sometimes Molly wondered whether his daughter found it odd that his hair was always damp at lunchtime, but she didn't ask. The last thing she wanted to do was to waste time checking up on the mechanics of how he was managing to keep the whole thing a secret.

She rolled over to face him, the sheet swathed around her body. 'Want some coffee?'

He propped himself up on one elbow. 'No.'

'You don't?'

'Not if it means you leaving this bed.'

'Then you'll have to go without, I'm afraid—I'm a little bit short of servants!'

He turned onto his back and stared at the ceiling, wondering what was troubling him. This should have been a dream scenario, and in a way it was. In bed with the most passionate woman he had ever known, with no questions asked and no demands made. The perfect no-strings affair and perfectly suited to Dimitri and his lifestyle.

He thought of the way her mouth had moved over his body only minutes earlier and some dark demon reared its head. He wondered how many conversations like this had taken place, with men like him. And when he was gone, how long would it take for her to replace him with another? A black wave of jealousy rose up to envelop him.

'Do you always bring your lovers here?' he asked.

Molly stilled. 'I'm sorry?'

He gave a faint, cynical smile. 'Prevaricating, Molly? You won't offend me, I can assure you. I simply asked whether you always brought your lovers here.'

She could only see his profile, stony and unyielding. 'What kind of a question is that?' she asked, in bewilderment.

He turned his head to look at her. 'You don't want to answer?'

'I don't think it's any of your business. I don't ask you about any of *your* lovers, do I?'

He shrugged. 'Ask away. What do you want to know?'

'That's the whole point—I don't want to know anything!'

'I don't believe you. Women are always curious.'

Maybe the women he usually slept with *were*, but maybe they were more used to playing this no-strings affair game than Molly was. Better equipped to deal with the inevitable outcome of such affairs. And besides, the questions she would liked to have asked him weren't 'Who?' or 'When?' or 'Where?' or 'How?' but the way they made him feel. And no answer he could give would ever satisfy her. 'Not this one,' she said stubbornly.

'Well, *I* am curious,' he murmured.

'Tough!' she said crossly. 'Is that how you get your kicks, then? Discussing who came before, and how much better you are at it than them?'

He smiled. 'Molly! You pay me a great compliment!'

'Oh, do shut up!'

He watched as she sat up and angrily tossed her head, the pale tumble of hair spilling down all over her shoulders. It was a gesture he had known so well and forgotten until this precise moment and he was disconcerted by it. 'You look like a goddess,' he whispered.

But she steeled her heart against his words. 'I bet you say that to all the girls!'

He frowned. 'Molly, you are very flippant.'

Well, of course she was—because what was the

alternative? Let a murmured compliment like that go to her head? Have her sighing and cooing and imagining it meant more than the fact that all he wanted was to make love to her again? Well, he could want in vain—she wasn't there to do his every bidding. She was an independent woman, and she was going to behave like one.

She threw the sheet aside and stepped out of bed.

'Where are you going?'

'To make some coffee. Would you like some?'

No, he would not like some, but he recognised the light of determination in her eyes. And besides, it was an entrancing spectacle to have a bristling, indignant Molly walking naked across the room. He lay back on the pillows and watched her. She moved like a dream, with her long, long legs and that high, firm bottom and rose-tipped breasts which were so lush.

'I can't think of anything I would prefer,' he said sardonically. She looked at him, and burst out laughing and he held his arms open. 'Molly,' he murmured. 'Come back to bed.'

'No!'

'Come on.'

It was terrible, but she did. Climbed back in and let him take her into his arms to feel the warm yielding of her flesh and the inevitable rush of heat.

He kissed her neck. 'You know you don't want coffee, *epikindhinos* Molly,' he whispered against her ear.

She closed her eyes. 'What's *epikindhinos*?'

'Look it up.'

'Tell me!'

'Dangerous,' he said slowly.

'Oh.' She quite liked that. He was dangerous, too.

He nibbled at her ear. 'Tell me about your books, then, if you don't want to tell me about your lovers.'

'Books?' She didn't want to talk about *anything*. She wanted him to make love to her again, and obliterate all the doubts and insecurities from her mind. 'What books?'

'What books?' He laughed. 'The books you write! Had you forgotten them?'

'Oh, those.'

'Yes,' he teased. 'Those.'

She had to frown to concentrate—almost as though she *had* forgotten, but then maybe she had. Her other life—her real life—seemed like a distant dream, a misty memory. As if the only life she had was the one here, in this bedroom, telescoped into the few short hours she saw him every day. Really saw him.

She didn't count the snatched glimpses, when she caught sight of him through the window, when he was returning having taken Zoe out somewhere. Then she would duck out of sight, afraid that he would think she had been watching out for him. Hiding back in the shadows of the curtain, like an obsessed woman with a guilty secret—which was crazy. She wasn't doing anything that she should be ashamed of, and neither was he—not really.

And if he had a somewhat over-developed and

protective attitude towards his daughter, then who was she to criticise? She couldn't really blame him for wanting to keep Zoe in the dark about their affair. Greek fathers ruled by example—and if he was seen to be having a casual affair with their next-door neighbour, then what kind of message would that send out to her? Especially as he was never going to see Molly again.

'I write books about different cities,' she said slowly. 'Especially for women. A woman's-eye view on a place, if you like. The kind of places they can go without getting harassed. The best hotels for women on their own, the places to visit and the places definitely *not* to visit, that kind of thing. I've done Rome and London and New York and San Francisco. Next month, I'm doing Paris.'

'But not Athens?' he mused.

She shook her head. 'No. Athens doesn't really have a big enough appeal. Most people just use it as a stepping-stone to get somewhere else—like the islands.'

'So why don't you write about Pondiki?'

'Because I won't write about anywhere that isn't already a tourist trap,' she said vehemently. 'Pondiki would be ruined if people discovered just how beautiful and unspoilt it was.'

He ran a fingertip across the tip of her breast and she shivered. 'You loved my island, didn't you, Molly?'

'Of course.' She stared at him as though it was a given, but her memories of it were all interwoven with her love for him. 'It is probably the most beautiful place I have ever visited in my life.' She closed her eyes, and could see it all quite clearly in her mind's eye. 'That blue, blue sea and all that soft white sand. Deserted beaches—'

'Not quite so deserted these days,' he put in. 'The tourists have discovered Pondiki's beauty for themselves. There are more people than you will remember.'

Molly opened her eyes and grimaced. 'You don't mean it's become *commercialised*, do you?'

He smiled at the expression of outrage on her face, then frowned. 'Fortunately, no. We saw mistakes being made elsewhere in the Aegean, and were determined not to follow them.'

'And how did you manage to do that?'

'A couple of us got together—and tied up most of the available land.'

'Your hotel must be doing well, then.'

There was a pause. 'Yes.'

'And who is running it while you're over here? At the very height of the season, too!' she teased.

Again, he hesitated, and Molly thought how uncharacteristic that was.

'My sisters' husbands are in charge,' he said. 'And two of my nephews.'

'Gosh, quite the little empire!'

He shot her a quick look. 'It's still a family-run business, Molly, the way it always was.'

'Don't frown,' she said lightly, and rubbed her finger against his brow.

He smiled as he stretched luxuriously, and flipped over onto his stomach. 'Make me relax, then.'

'You want me to massage your back?'

'And the rest.'

'You'll have to turn onto your back if you want *that*!'

He turned over again, and looked at her through narrowed eyes. She was so generous, so giving of her body. She gave with as much pleasure as she received. He groaned as she began to tiptoe her fingers up his leg, and beyond.

'Molly, where the hell did you learn how to do that?'

'No questions, Dimitri. Remember?'

'Yes,' he groaned. 'I remember.'

There was silence for a while, until he moaned softly as her mouth worked its sweet magic, and then he pinned her back onto the bed and kissed her where she was moist and soft and warm, until she bucked and called his name out loud, in a cry that went on and on. He sent a wry look towards the open window and Molly saw it, pushing her hair back from her flushed face.

'I made a lot of noise.'

He smiled. 'A little.'

'It's a good thing Zoe isn't there.'

'Yes. Speaking of which…I'd better get going.'

'Better had,' she agreed lightly. 'She'll be back soon.'

He glanced at her. 'You think I'm an over-protective father?'

'I think you're a very *Greek* father.'

'Which doesn't answer my question.'

'How can I possibly say what you are or what you aren't, Dimitri? I've never been a parent, so I haven't got an earthly clue.'

'So why not?' he asked suddenly. 'Why not a parent?'

She stilled. 'Oh, you know…things.'

'What things?' He lifted her fingertips to his lips and began to tease them with his teeth. 'I don't know unless you tell me.'

'Is it relevant?'

'Mmm?' The nip became a kiss. 'To what?'

'To us. To what we have.' Oh, Lord—did that sound as though she was building it into something it wasn't? 'I mean, do you really need to know?'

'On a need-to-know basis,' he reflected thoughtfully, 'no. I don't. But I would like to know. Is that not natural? You cannot compartmentalise an affair to the extent that it's just no-holds barred sex and off limits for everything else.'

But wasn't that exactly what he usually did? Didn't he normally steer clear of any line of questioning which might throw up emotion? And didn't the fact that he was breaking one of his own rules spell out the word he had used to her earlier? *Epikindhinos.*

She shook her head. She felt vulnerable and exposed and not just because she was lying naked in bed next to him. She hadn't expected him to ask questions like that, and certainly not now. How could you talk about the non-fulfilment of your dreams in a few snatched moments? 'We haven't got time for this discussion,' she said, looking pointedly at the clock. 'You've got to go.'

It was rather ironic that because she was virtually ordering him to leave, he wanted to do the exact opposite. How contrary was human nature? he wondered wryly. He was more accustomed to the scenario of women begging him to stay. Elusiveness could be very provocative indeed—but ultimately, he reminded himself, it was all just a game played between the sexes.

He went into the shower, using the soap and shampoo he had installed in there, telling Molly that it might arouse suspicions if he went home smelling of lavender!

Yet it was crazy, it was as if he were leaving something of himself here. Some kind of territorial marking. His soap. His shampoo. Bizarre, or just expedient? Because this wasn't an affair like any other he'd had, was it? The normal rules did not apply, which was maybe why he seemed to be breaking them. She lived next door, and his daughter was with him.

And he knew her.

Or did he?

Did the past have more powerful tentacles than you gave it credit for? Playing tricks with your memory and with time itself—so that it seemed easy to shrug off today, and to lose yourself in part of yesterday?

How much of the eighteen-year-old Molly remained in her today, any more than the eighteen-year-old Dimitri did in him? How much of character was formed then, and how much evolved by the trials and the hurdles you had to leap over in life? He had had an explosive sexual compatibility with Molly then, and that much had not changed. She had always been able to make him laugh, and that much had not changed either.

But she had always been able to infuriate him, too—and to drive him wild with a jealousy which raged like a black demon inside him. He had always put that down to the difference in their respective upbringings, but maybe it was something more fundamental than that.

Just to look at her was to want to possess her, and that kind of possession constrained and tied you in a way in which he did not want to be tied. A way which was incompatible with life as he liked to live it.

'Have you drowned in there?' she called from the bedroom.

'Yeah—come and give me mouth-to-mouth resuscitation!'

He walked back into the room, tiny droplets of water still drying on his naked body, rubbing a towel at the wet ebony hair, and his mouth hardened when he saw her.

She had put on some oversized towelling robe. A man's? It made her look a beguiling mix of innocence and sensuality, and she had made a tray of coffee which was scenting the air with its bitter, pungent aroma.

It was a scene which mocked a domesticity they would never have, the kind of cosy scene which should have sent him running straight out of the door.

He pulled on his boxer shorts and Molly thought how incredibly beautiful he was, how graceful for such a big, strong man.

He looked up to find her watching him and something he read in her eyes made his mouth dry, until he remembered. 'It's the weekend,' he stated flatly.

She looked up from the steaming cafetière. 'So it is,' she said lightly.

'And I won't be able to see you until Monday.'

'No. That's right.' She had been practising for just this moment. 'Planning to do anything special?'

He frowned. She was rewriting the script, and he didn't like it. She might have had the finesse to look even a *little* bit disappointed.

'You're frowning again,' she teased.

He ignored that. 'Are *you*?' he questioned. 'Planning to do something special?'

Well, what did he expect? That she would be sitting around the place mooning over him? Hoping to catch a brief, furtive glimpse of him over the garden wall—their eyes sending silent, frustrated messages? Gazing with longing as he took Zoe off somewhere?

'I'm going to a gallery tomorrow afternoon, and then out to dinner with some friends in the evening.'

'Oh. Which gallery is that?'

'Tate Britain. They've got a huge exhibition of Rembrandt—it's supposed to be quite something.'

'Maybe Zoe might like to go along. She likes art.'

Molly raised her eyebrows at him. 'And accidentally bump into each other, you mean?'

'Why not?'

'Because it's dishonest, that's why,' she found herself saying. 'It's pretending to be something it's not. A casual meeting—which isn't casual at all! And maybe she might pick up on the fact that we're...' Lord, but it was a struggle to find socially acceptable words for a no-strings relationship! 'More friendly than neighbours usually are.'

He gave a faint smile. 'What a delightful way to describe it.'

'Perhaps you could come up with a better description?' she questioned sweetly.

He looked at her with frustrated admiration. Had he thought that this would be easy? With *Molly*? The getting her into bed had been a piece of cake, but she was somehow managing the impossible—of being more intimate than he felt entirely comfortable with, while managing to hold him at arm's length!

'Look, maybe we could have lunch on Monday?' he suggested.

'Where, here?'

'No, not here!' he exploded. Anywhere but here! Nowhere within a fifty-metre radius of a bed! 'There must be a restaurant, locally.'

'Of course there is.'

'Well, then.'

'What about Zoe? What will you tell her?'

'Oh, Zoe has made friends with another Greek girl. She can go back with her after school, she'd like that. We'll have lunch on Monday—how's that?'

How *was* that? Well, considering he had simply asked her out for a meal, her heart was pounding with the kind of excitement she couldn't remember feeling in a long, long time. Was he finding the trysts in her spare room claustrophobic? she wondered. Already?

'I'll book it, shall I?'

He began to button up his shirt and nodded. 'Book it,' he agreed.

'And you'll come round here first?'

He saw the fire of sensual hunger which lit her eyes from within, and smiled. He knew what she meant, come round and go to bed with her first.

'No. I'll pick you up just before one,' he said coolly.

CHAPTER SEVEN

THE small Italian restaurant was noisy and crowded and the waiter greeted Molly with a beaming look of surprise. *'Signora!'* he exclaimed. 'It is too long! Where have you been?'

Molly smiled back. 'Oh, I've been around,' she said. 'Just busy, that's all.'

'My sister—I send her your book all about Roma!'

'But she lives there, Marco,' said Molly seriously as she took her seat. 'Why would she want a guide-book?'

'Because my sister, she not like my mother! She and her friends—they like to go places without men, and your book tell her where.'

'Your English is improving,' said Molly diplomatically.

He shrugged. 'My girlfriend is Italian. We don't speak English.'

Dimitri took the menu he had been offered with a thin smile. Perhaps she should invite the waiter to draw up a chair!

Molly leaned forward. 'What would you like to drink, Dimitri? This meal is on me.'

He went as still as if she had suddenly leapt up on the table and started dancing on it. 'You are not pay-ing,' he said flatly.

'Oh, yes, I am,' she contradicted and saw the glower on his face. 'For heaven's sake! Think of all the meals you bought me on Pondiki!'

'You had little money—you were a student.'

'And now I do, and I'm not a student any more. People often go Dutch, these days.'

'I have never been bought lunch by a woman,' he said darkly.

'Then why not try it?' Her eyes glittered. 'You could be in for a treat.' She shook her head as she saw his expression. 'I thought you might have moved a bit more with the times.'

It was difficult to shrug off an attitude which had been ingrained in him. 'I will buy lunch today,' he stated unequivocally. 'To repay you for your party. Next time, you can do it.'

She opened her mouth to object and shut it again, seeing from the resolute look in his dark eyes that to object would be pointless. And wasn't there a stupid side of her which loved the mastery which spilled over into all other aspects of his life? You didn't get to be such a consummate lover as Dimitri without some of the arrogant assurance he was demonstrating right now.

'Champagne?' he questioned.

'Are we celebrating something?'

'I thought you liked champagne.'

'Yes, I do. Thank you.'

Marco brought over the bottle, poured them two glasses and stood waiting for their order for food, though for once Molly lacked her usual enthusiastic appetite for the delicious Italian food she could smell.

'Know what you want?' asked Dimitri, with a quick look at the menu.

'The same as you,' she said.

He raised his eyebrows only fractionally and then proceeded to give their order in fluent and seamless Italian and, after Marco had gone, Molly leaned back in her chair, cradling her cold champagne and looking at him ruefully.

'I'd forgotten you spoke Italian.'

'And Spanish,' he reminded her arrogantly.

'Must be handy for lovers, being able to converse in their tongue!'

'I prefer to converse with *my* tongue,' he said wickedly, touching his glass to hers and enjoying her furious blush.

'That was completely uncalled for!'

'You started it,' he pointed out. 'Are we going to argue our entire way through lunch?'

'No.'

'Then stop sulking.'

'I'm not.'

'Yes, you are—do you mind telling me why?'

It would be completely outrageous to tell him the truth, surely? 'You didn't even kiss me when you picked me up.'

'Ah.' He removed the glass from between her fingers and put it on the table and placed his own next to it, then enfolded her hand between both of his instead. 'You know why?'

'No, I don't.'

'Because when I kiss you, it drives me crazy. It makes me want to take all your clothes off and to make long, slow and passionate love to you.' His eyes glittered. 'Or hard, fast passionate love to you!'

Her fingernails bit into the palm of his hand. 'Dimitri, stop it,' she urged desperately.

'Am I making you want me?' he teased.

'You know you are.'

He let go of her hand and put the champagne back. 'Drink this instead.'

'I'll be as high as a kite!'

'On one glass?'

She didn't like to tell him that she felt high already, before she had taken even a single sip. But that was the effect he had on her, and maybe she didn't have to tell him. Maybe he knew.

And besides, his physical effect on her wasn't what was in question, was it? So what was? Their compatibility outside the bedroom? No. Lovers didn't need to be compatible—they just needed to be able to get through the occasional restaurant meal, for propriety's sake, without falling straight into bed.

'Look, here comes our starter!' she said.

'Oh, good,' he said drily.

She pushed a bit of Parma ham around on her plate. 'Look,' she said conversationally. 'It's so thinly sliced that you can see the plate through it.'

'Are we going to make small talk?' he asked.

She looked up, the unwanted ham forgotten. 'So

that's no arguing and no small talk. Could be a bit limiting, Dimitri. What do you want to talk about?'

He glowered at the piece of melon on his fork, comparing it to its infinitely sweeter and more succulent Pondiki equivalent. What did he want? Why, perversely, when he avoided in-depth conversation like the plague—did he find himself wanting one with Molly?

Because the past made them comfortable together, and he wanted to catch up. And Molly was sensible and liberated enough not to read anything into it— why, it had been *her* who had suggested the 'no strings', hadn't it? And taken the wind right out of his sails into the bargain.

'Tell me about your marriage,' he said suddenly.

'My *marriage*?' She blinked at him. 'Why would you want to know about that?' Had she thought— hoped—that he would be jealous of Hugo?

'I am interested to hear about the man who won your heart.'

It seemed a curious way for him to describe it— an overly romantic description which seemed a world away from the cynical man who sat in front of her. Maybe that was true for him and Malantha—but it was certainly not true for her.

'Don't you know that you can never get an objective opinion on someone from their ex-spouse?'

'Do you hate him, then?'

She shook her head. 'Oh, no, I don't hate him. It makes it all seem so pointless if I do that—anyway, there's nothing to hate.' And that had been part of the problem. She had felt all the *right* things about Hugo—all the things she had thought you were supposed to feel about the man with whom you wanted to spend the rest of your life. Respect, liking, admiration. All those worthy qualities which turned out not to be worth anything when they weren't laced together with a healthy dose of passion.

But Molly had been frightened of passion. She had seen the stormy extremes it could provoke in her. And men might initially be attracted to a passionate woman, but in the end they chose the quieter, calmer, safer option for a lifetime commitment. Look at Dimitri and Malantha.

So she had quelled her passion, though that had been easy with Hugo. It had been her mind he had fallen in love with, or so he had said. And although at the time she had been immensely flattered by that, it had not been a strong enough glue to cement an honest relationship between a man and a woman.

'We were complete opposites, really,' she said slowly. 'He kept my feet on the ground and I guess I helped him let his hair down a bit. I admired his steadiness, and he liked my get-up-and-go.'

'So what was he like?'

It was tempting to say that he was as unlike Dimitri as possible, but she didn't. What would that say about why they were sitting here together today?

'Quiet. Bookish. Clever,' she said slowly.

'He doesn't sound your type.'

'Thanks.' She pursed her lips together in a wry

smile. 'Which bit? The clever? The quiet? Or maybe even the bookish?'

'I did not mean that. It is not a very flattering way for a man to be described,' he observed.

'What would that be, then?' she challenged. 'Rampant stud?'

His eyes grew steely and cold. 'Is that how you see me, then, *agape mou*?' he questioned silkily.

'Well, partly,' she said truthfully. 'But you're clever, too. But I didn't come out for lunch to compare you to my ex-husband.'

'No.' He sat back while Marco took their plates away. 'Did he want children?'

She bit her lip. 'Dimitri, that's an incredibly personal question!'

He leaned forward and took her hand again, rubbing it softly with the pad of his thumb. 'You don't think that what the two of us have been doing together entitles us to ask questions like that?'

She shrugged. Wasn't he in danger of confusing sexual intimacy with *real* intimacy? But when she thought about it—why shouldn't she tell him? Her desires would not affect him, and anyway—he had a daughter of his own and she was very nearly grown up.

'We talked about having children, of course—in that vague, hopeful way that you do when you get married. And of course, we always put it off for various reasons—you know, we wanted a bigger house, and then we had to remortgage the house to start the business. Then we worked all hours to get the business up and running, and when we could finally afford to have them we looked around and realised that we didn't love one another any more.'

'Just like that?' he echoed sardonically.

'Well, no, of course not. We tried going to counselling, but that didn't work, and I think we were about to call it a day when Hugo fell in love with someone else and that, in a funny kind of way, seemed to make it easier.'

'And he married her?'

'No, but they live together. Both of them think that marriage is an overrated and outdated institution and neither of them want children.'

'And do you...?' He paused for a moment and nodded his thanks to Marco who had removed their starters and replaced them with two steaming plates of chicken and pasta which he suspected that neither of them would touch. 'And do you think it an outdated institution, Molly?'

'Of course,' she said lightly. 'Unless you have children, of course—then it's different.' He was topping her glass up; she hadn't even realised that she had finished the first, and maybe that was what gave her the courage to ask her next question, even though he had been quite open about quizzing her about *her* marriage. But then, *her* marriage wouldn't give him any pain, would it? And that was where the imbalance lay.

'What was your marriage like, Dimitri?'

He had known that this was coming, and she had been honest enough with him, but it was still difficult to talk about. 'I guess it was over almost before it began—we barely had any time together,' he said quietly. 'It seems such a long time ago now.' He was quiet for a moment. 'It was. A very long time. There was so much adjustment, to life as man and wife—and then to becoming parents.'

'It must have been…hard. Not to have had much time together as a couple.'

'Yes.' His expression was one of acceptance. 'But it was the way things were.'

'And Malantha?'

He smiled. 'Malantha was sweet and sound and she adored me.'

Somehow she got the words out, telling herself that she had no right to be jealous, no right at all. 'And you adored her too, presumably?'

'Yes, I did,' he said simply. 'She was easy. Comfortable. No stress. No worries.'

She wanted to say to him, Then *why me*? Why, if you adored each other so much, did you make love to me and take my heart and then break it up into tiny little pieces? But she did not say it. Now she understood that passion could be separated from the common goal that he and Malantha had shared. And maybe he guessed at her unasked question, for he seemed to answer it with his next words.

'We had grown up together,' he explained. 'We shared the same experiences, the same hopes, the same dreams. We wanted a big family—lots of children running around, brought up with the same values that we had known.'

It was so different from the world she had been brought up in, and for the first time Molly was able to see that what had happened had perhaps happened for a reason. For what would have been the alternative?

Just say, just say that Dimitri had loved her as deeply as she was sure she had loved him. Thinking it through—did she really think it would have worked if the fairy-tale scenario had come true? Her as his young bride, her studies abandoned. Living in a starkly different culture with people who were hostile towards everything she stood for?

The scales fell from her eyes and the realisation brought with it a sadness—for seeing youthful dreams for what they were was always sad—but also a regenerating kind of freedom.

'Go on,' she said softly.

'But what we both wanted was not to be. Fate had other plans for us.'

She wanted to stroke his hand, to tell him that she was so terribly, terribly sorry, but she knew that it would be the most inappropriate thing of all, so instead she said nothing. His deep, silken voice sounded very distant.

'And unlike you, there were no reasons to put off having children. We think that Malantha became pregnant on our honeymoon....'

He seemed reluctant to continue, but something made her prompt him; she didn't know what, because the honeymoon bit had hurt like hell and there was doubtless worse to follow. But not for her. For him. 'Go on,' she said, again.

Her words barely registered. 'It was a…difficult pregnancy. Malantha needed a Caesarian and they had to send a helicopter to Crete. She…she took a long time to come round after the operation—the anaesthetic had affected her badly. They said that might have been a contributing factor.'

There was a pause and Molly scarcely breathed. Suddenly the hubbub and jollity of the lively restaurant faded into nothing. All she could see and hear was the man with the pain etched on his face and in his voice.

'She suffered a pulmonary embolism,' he said finally. 'And when Zoe was just three days old, she died.'

This time she did take his hand. She didn't care what he thought. Sometimes human beings needed comfort, proper physical, tactile comfort. She squeezed his fingers and he looked at her, his eyes clearing, like someone who was coming out of a bad place.

'I've never told that to anyone before,' he said simply. 'Not since it happened.'

She could imagine. He had needed to be strong. For the new baby. For his family and, presumably, for Malantha's family too, who must have been heartbroken. And who could the strong, capable Dimitri Nicharos possibly confide in? Who would he dare confide in, for fear of appearing weak, and less of a man? His tears must have been shed in private, his grief borne alone.

And suddenly his behaviour became understandable. Who could blame him if since then he had avoided commitment? If he compartmentalised his pleasure so that it would not intrude on the close and loving unit he had built up with his daughter?

Her own worries and fears became puny and insignificant in comparison. She lifted his hand to her mouth and kissed it, very, very gently.

'Malantha would be so proud and so pleased if she could see Zoe now,' she said softly. 'I mean, I've only spoken to her once, but she seems polite and sensible. And she is just so very beautiful.'

He smiled. 'Yes. And she's pretty bright, too. She wants to become a doctor.'

'That's a long, hard training,' she observed.

'I know. But she's had her heart set on it since she was a little girl.'

Suddenly she badly wanted to be on her own with him. 'Dimitri, shall we go?'

He withdrew his hand. Picked up his glass of champagne and drained it in one. Then glanced at his watch. 'No pudding?'

'I'm not hungry.'

'No.' Their eyes met. 'Me neither.'

'You can...pay the bill if you really want to,' she said.

'Is that a climb-down?' he questioned.

'Of sorts.'

His eyes smiled. 'Or split it?'

'Okay,' she said breathlessly. 'We'll split it.'

It felt like a victory of sorts, and when they walked out into the bright summer day he caught her in his arms, so tightly that she had to struggle to breathe.

His expression was fierce when he looked down at her. 'Do you know what I'm going to do now, Molly Garcia?'

She shook her head, even though she had a pretty good idea. But she wanted to be told.

He put his mouth to her ear. 'I am going to take you home and undress you and make you undress me and then I will spend the rest of the afternoon making love to you until you beg me to stop.'

'And what if I don't?'

'Then I won't stop.'

She shivered with excitement and an almost unbearable sense of expectation and she had the courage to link her arm through his. Until they turned the corner into the street and she removed it like a person snatching their hand from a fire.

'Oh, Lord,' she moaned.

For there, walking towards them from the opposite direction, was Zoe.

CHAPTER EIGHT

DIMITRI said something very softly in Greek.

'What shall we do?' hissed Molly.

And something in her frantic tone told him that this was all in danger of getting out of hand. 'We're neighbours, remember? Neighbours can go out and eat lunch together,' he said. 'Act normally.'

What was normal at a time like this?

She smiled rather helplessly at Zoe, who didn't seem at all fazed to see her walking side by side with her father.

'Papa!' She smiled her blindingly beautiful smile. 'Hello, Molly!'

Dimitri looked at his daughter and frowned. 'I thought I was due to collect you later this evening, from Cara's house?'

'I changed my mind.' Zoe shrugged. 'Cara had a boy round.'

'A *boy*?' exploded Dimitri. 'What boy?'

Zoe sighed. 'Just a friend of Cara's, Papa.'

'Where is he now?'

Zoe began to look alarmed. 'Papa, it's nothing. Really.' She shot Molly an agonised look as if to say, Help me!

'Don't you think you're overreacting a little, Dimitri?' said Molly mildly. 'She *is* getting on for

115

sixteen.' He shot her a furious look and she realised that she had said too much. A neighbour would never have started dishing out advice to a man like Dimitri unless they knew one another very well. She just hoped that Zoe wouldn't guess how well.

'Where have *you* been, Papa?' Zoe asked.

'Don't change the subject!' he thundered. 'How did you get home?'

'On the bus.'

'The *bus!*'

'Papa, *everyone* takes the bus.'

'Not my daughter! You should have taken a taxi!'

They drew up outside Molly's house and she let out a small sigh of relief. 'Well, time I was going,' she said. 'Nice to see you again, Zoe. Call round any time you like, you're very welcome.'

'Thank you,' said Zoe.

'Bye, Dimitri,' said Molly casually. She lifted her face to his, wondering if he would send a silent see-you-tomorrow message with his eyes, but his eyes were as coolly distant as if they had just been introduced for the first time. No, cooler than that—positively icy. So was he angry with *her*? For being caught with her in the first place? Or was he thinking that she had interfered by trying to intervene when he was arguing with Zoe?

Well, damn you, she thought as she let herself into the house. She thought about all the sad things he had told her and the way he had coped but that didn't change a thing. He could not and should not get off with behaviour like that. Just because you had had to cope with terrible tragedy in your life, it didn't give you carte blanche to treat people as though they had no feelings to hurt.

She wondered did he think he would just stroll round tomorrow and she let him, and that they would go straight upstairs and undress and make mad, passionate love and then off he would go, his face a study of innocence.

Then he was wrong.

What had she been thinking of? To imagine that she could tolerate such a 'relationship' with a man to whom she had once been so close. Accepting whatever scraps he saw fit to throw at her. To settle for so little from someone who had once meant the world to her.

Deliberately, Molly set her alarm clock early, showering and dressing to be out of the house by eight, when she knew that Dimitri and Zoe would be at breakfast.

She walked up to Hampstead village where she went shopping for clothes she neither wanted nor needed. Forcing herself to go through the mechanics of trying on skirts and T-shirts and dresses. Sifting through the sale racks with a lacklustre hand until she came away from them empty-handed.

She went to a pavement café and sat outside drinking a cappuccino, but the world seemed full of lovers that morning. Real lovers, mocking her with their open displays of affection—not lovers hiding away, as if they were doing something wrong and shameful.

She browsed in a bookshop and bought a couple

of paperbacks she had been meaning to read for ages and ate a Caesar salad for lunch in the adjoining restaurant. And only at two o'clock, when she was certain that Zoe would be home and that Dimitri wouldn't dare come round—God forbid!—did she wend her way home.

But she was just putting her key into the front door lock when she heard a silky dark voice behind her.

'Hello, Molly.'

She didn't look round. 'Careful, Dimitri,' she said sarcastically. 'We could be seen! Even now, there could be paparazzi lurking in the bushes waiting to capture us for all eternity.' She opened the door and turned to face him, but he pushed her inside and closed the door shut behind them.

'What the hell do you think you're doing?'

He steadied his breathing, tempted to kiss her, but he did not want to seduce her into rational thinking. If she couldn't think straight without being in his arms, then what was the point? For an uncomplicated 'no strings' affair, things certainly didn't seem to be going according to plan!

'Where were you this morning?'

'That's none of your business.'

'I thought we had an arrangement.'

'Oh, did you? You mean another surreptitious assignation? I'm surprised you were afraid to risk it after nearly being caught out yesterday!'

'Molly…Zoe knows.'

Her eyes flashed. 'Knows what…exactly?'

'She saw us coming down the road together and

she came to the conclusion that we were in some way…involved.'

Clever Zoe. 'But she doesn't know that we were…lovers…all those years ago?'

He shook his head. 'No. On a need-to-know basis, I didn't think that was necessary.'

'And was she shocked? Horrified?'

'No.' In fact, his daughter's reaction had surprised him. He had a couple of male friends—one American and one English—who had told him that their offspring had made their lives a living hell when they had become involved with other women. Though maybe it was different for divorcees, than for widowers, he reflected.

Far from being angry, or jealous, or appalled at the thought of her 'Papa' seeing a woman, Zoe had given him a lecture on how it was about time and that he was only thirty-four and should not behave like a hermit. That you only had one life to live and that she thought it was a good idea he had started to go out with women, and that she gave him her blessing.

Her blessing!

He had sat there, bemused, listening to the oddly mature speech from his daughter and wondering when she had started to grow up so much, and how had he come to miss it along the way?

He shrugged, and suddenly he looked about eighteen again and all the fight went out of Molly and she put her arms around him, put her cheek next to his.

'I'm sorry,' she whispered.

'No, I'm the one who should be sorry.'

'Shall we toss for it? Whoever wins is the sorriest?'

He started laughing and he put his arms tight around her waist. 'Ah, Molly,' he sighed and kissed the tip of her nose. 'Tell me what is it that you want from me?'

She didn't answer for a moment. He would expect, and he would receive, a calm, considered response, not some emotional outpouring of impossible desire from a woman old enough and experienced enough to know better.

She took a deep breath. 'There's nothing wrong with what we have. An affair suits me fine.'

'It does?'

'Sure. Why not? It's just all this secrecy stuff I don't like.'

'Well, there is no need for secrecy; not now. Zoe knows.'

'I know she does—but that doesn't really change anything. I mean, you can't just come round and disappear inside and the blinds come down and two hours later—hey, presto!—you're back again! Can you? Where is she now, by the way?'

'She and Cara have gone to the cinema.'

Her heart leapt, and she cursed it. 'She may be mature, but she's still your daughter—and daughters are notoriously bad at recognising that their fathers are entitled to some kind of sex-life.'

He winced slightly at the baldness of her statement. Sex-life. But what she said was true, wasn't it? Did that sum up what they had? All they had?

'And quite rightly so.' Molly shuddered as she continued. 'I could never bear to think of my own mother and father doing it—I mean, who can?'

His smile was indulgent as he ran the flat of his hand down over the pale, blonde sheet of hair which tumbled down past her shoulders.

'Molly, Molly, Molly. You want that we should do other things? More exciting things?'

She widened her eyes deliberately. 'Just what *are* you suggesting, Dimitri? Swinging from the chandeliers? Bondage?'

'Molly!' he protested. 'Be serious!'

But she didn't dare. Keeping it light and flippant meant that she could keep the whole thing in perspective. He might feel bad about the furtiveness and the secrecy, but that didn't mean that he was suddenly pulling another, more committed option out, did it—like a magician pulling out a rabbit from a hat?

'I'd just like to do some other stuff,' she said. 'Apart from the bed bit.'

'What kind of stuff?'

She moved her shoulders restlessly. 'Oh, you know—normal stuff. Walks in the park, that kind of thing. Taking a boat down the river. Everyday things which are so much fun.' She saw an odd kind of expression on his face. 'What is it?'

'You don't want to go shopping?' he said drily.

'You don't want jewels, or designer clothes and meals in fancy hotels?'

She understood the implication immediately, but she wasn't tempted or seduced by it. She had always been happy with the simple things in life—especially with him. 'Is that what women usually want from you, then?'

'They try. Women are fond of symbols, and status.'

'Well, I hope you don't give in to them,' she said crossly, any jealousy of the other women in his life momentarily eclipsed by indignation that her own sex could behave in such an outrageously mercenary way. 'You may have a share in a gorgeous hotel on a Greek island, but that doesn't make you Rockefeller!'

He gave a comfortable, lazy smile. 'I never give what is asked for; gifts should only ever be given freely. Come, Molly.' He kissed the tips of her fingers. 'It is a beautiful day. Let us go and find your park.'

But she shook her head. 'No, not today,' she whispered and she coiled her fingers into the rich, ebony silk of his hair, pulling him towards her so that she could feel the hard, sinewy jut of his hips. 'Today I want you to take me to bed.'

He groaned. 'But you just said...'

'I know I did. But I'm a woman, Dimitri and I'm entitled to change my mind. If you'd tried to take me to bed, I'd have wanted to go to the park.'

'There's only one way to shut you up, Molly Garcia,' he murmured.

'And what's that?' she questioned innocently, but she knew what the answer was even before he began to kiss her.

'That?' he murmured into her mouth.

'That,' she agreed.

He pulled his mouth away and smiled and she looked up at him, feeling oddly shy, as if all her defences had somehow been stripped away, leaving her vulnerable and open. He planted a kiss on each eyelid. Small, sweet kisses which ensnared her more than the deep demonstration of passion might have done. Left her shaking inside.

'You want to take me upstairs?' he questioned.

'I—I guess.'

He followed her upstairs and they removed their clothes swiftly, almost clinically, as if they couldn't wait to be rid of them, then they lay on the bed and he felt her soft sigh as their warm flesh met, and he ran a reflective finger around her mouth.

'Wouldn't it be great to spend a night together?' she blurted out, then saw his face close and wished she could unsay it.

'And maybe we will,' he said idly. But he never spent a night with a woman. If you slept with a woman it put things on a different footing—a too-intimate footing. The little things like brushing teeth and taking a bath together—somehow those things spelt danger. Took things onto a different sphere.

'Oh, I'm not fussed,' she said convincingly. 'You probably snore!'

He smiled at this and then bent his head to kiss her. And kiss her and kiss her and kiss her.

'Dimitri,' she gasped, against his mouth.

'Ne?' But his tongue flicked sensuously inside her mouth.

'Dimitri,' she said again, indistinctly.

'What is it, *agape mou*?'

'Oh, Dimitri,' she half sobbed. 'Dimitri!'

Now she was squirming against him, her body inviting him into hers in unspoken plea and he made a little imprecation against her mouth, slipping his hand between her thighs, feeling her hot and slick and ready. This was not how he had planned it. He had planned to take for ever, but it seemed that for ever would now never come. He was powerless, he realised helplessly, as with a small moan he entered her.

Afterwards, they lay in silence for a while, and Molly was sure that Dimitri had fallen asleep, when he spoke.

'So maybe you might like to come round to my house?'

She sat up in bed, frowning, looking down at his face to properly understand what he meant. 'You mean, to go to bed there?'

'No. Very definitely not to go to bed there. But as Zoe knows we are…friends—'

'Interesting choice of word, Dimitri,' she commented drily.

'There seems no reason why you shouldn't meet socially.'

It sounded like the opposite to taking someone home to meet their parents, thought Molly, slightly hysterically.

'And she should mix with more English people,' he added.

Well, that very definitely let her know where she stood! When she wasn't making love to the father, she could engage in polite conversation with his daughter!

'Sounds good to me,' she said steadily.

'Why don't you come round for tea, next Saturday?' he suggested casually.

'I'd...I'd love to.'

Which was how Molly found herself next door sipping Earl Grey tea the following Saturday, with Dimitri and his daughter, in the sunny sitting room which mirrored her own.

Zoe *was* very bright—almost precociously so, thought Molly—but she seemed eager to talk about all the kinds of things which girls of that age invariably did. Fashion, mainly. She was going to be a very elegant doctor, thought Molly ruefully as she eyed her linen crop-trousers and a matching little top which showed off a perfectly flat midriff.

Molly was just telling her about the latest outrageously expensive designer shop in Notting Hill, where all the season's must-have clothes were, when the telephone rang and Dimitri threw them both a questioning look. 'Seems like I'm pretty superfluous to requirements,' he commented with a smile. 'That's a call I've been expecting—mind if I deal with it?'

'Oh, no, Papa,' said Zoe quickly. 'Take as long as you like.'

'I think I can just about take a hint as big as that one,' he said drily.

But the fashion-fest dried up just as soon as he had left the room, and Zoe put her cup down.

'Molly?'

Molly smiled. 'Zoe?'

'You are close to my father, yes?'

Tricky. 'Well, we have become friends.' And that was the truth. 'Why?'

Zoe sighed, her beautiful full mouth expressively turning down at the corners. 'He thinks I am going to be a doctor.'

'Well, that's because you *are* going to be a doctor. Aren't you?'

Zoe shook her head, the thick black hair which hung almost to her waist swaying like a pair of satin curtains around her oval face, and for one brief moment Molly saw Malantha sitting there. 'I don't want to. Not any more.'

'That's okay,' said Molly easily. 'Lots of girls change their minds about their career choices. What did you have in mind instead?'

There was a pause. 'I want to be a model.'

And then Molly understood. Or rather, she saw it how Dimitri would see it. 'Oh, Zoe—are you sure? It's such a competitive world. I mean, I think you're very, very beautiful—well, you are—and I'm sure you've got what it takes. But there are hundreds of girls out there who want to be models.'

Zoe nodded. 'I know this. But an agent in America has given me a card.'

'Do you *know* him?' asked Molly worriedly.

'Her,' corrected Zoe with a smile. 'The agent was a woman. I am not stupid. I checked the agency out and her credentials. It is one of the top agencies in the world. I can earn a lot of money, Molly. And see the world.'

'Are you quite sure you've changed your mind about medicine?'

'Yes.' Zoe nodded her head with firm resolution. 'Once, I cherished that dream, but no more. I don't want to do it any more, and I have to make Papa understand that. He is so…*old-fashioned*…with me. He hates me wearing make-up and he hates me seeing boys, even as friends.'

'Maybe he's just trying to protect you,' suggested Molly gently.

'But I would never do anything to lose my father's respect,' declared Zoe. 'He has to realise I'm growing up, and I must be free to choose how I live my own life.' There was a pause. 'And you can help me, Molly.'

Molly shook her head. 'Oh, no. No. Definitely, no. I have absolutely no influence over your father. Why would he listen to me?'

'Because you have talked to me. Tell him that I have thought it through—that it is not just some mad idea of a young woman. I can be a successful model,

I know that.' She struck her hand over her heart. 'In here.'

Molly smiled. Youthful passion—how clear and yet how blind it could be! 'Can't you tell him that yourself?'

'He will not listen to me. Our roles are too clearly defined, Molly—surely you can see that?'

'What about someone back home? Another woman who knows you both well? Someone you can confide in?'

Zoe shook her head. 'There is no one. Papa's sisters would think the same as him. They all treat me as a child. And sometimes it is better if an outsider steps in, you know? What is it that you say? They have no axe to grind.'

She really *was* a clever girl, thought Molly. Her assessment was accurate and true, if painful. The outsider. Yes.

But she sighed, unable to steel her heart against the look of appeal in the huge black eyes. Hard to believe that she had only been a few years older than her when she had first met Dimitri. Then she had thought she had known everything, just as Zoe did now.

'I'm not promising anything,' she said.

'Just promise you'll speak to him,' begged Zoe. 'That's all.'

All? Did she have no comprehension of the formidable will of her father? It was at that moment that Molly realised just how young Zoe was. 'Okay,' she said reluctantly. 'I promise.'

CHAPTER NINE

MOLLY'S face was thoughtful as she brushed her hair, clouds of newly washed blonde hair surrounding her face like a halo.

Dimitri watched her reflection in the mirror. 'Deep thoughts?' he asked.

Of course. All good things came to an end. There was a season for everything. He was going tomorrow and although she had resolutely tried not to think about it, sometimes her resolution failed her.

'Just thinking,' she said.

'About tomorrow?'

'No, about my tax return!'

He laughed, but it was a laugh edged with regret. Things changed. People changed. You could never predict the outcome of anything, he knew that. All he *did* know was that tomorrow he would be heading back to *his* world and leaving Molly in hers.

'It has been wonderful, Molly,' he began slowly, but she shook her head, so that the blonde hair flailed from her head, like the rays of the sun.

'No!' she said quietly. 'I don't want to go there. I don't want to spend our last few hours talking about what's happened, in the past tense. It *has* been lovely, yes. It was what it was, so let's just leave it at that, shall we?'

He pulled a shirt on. If this was one of those unspoken ultimatums, then she had better understand that he would not be forced in a corner. 'Sure.'

But Molly's nerves had been on edge this morning for another reason, too. She had made a promise to Zoe and she could not put it off any longer.

'Dimitri, I don't quite know how to say this.'

He stilled, his senses on alert. Here it came: the ultimatum. 'Say what, *agape*?' he queried, his eyes warning her not to say anything which she would regret.

Molly read the message and took heed of it, even though she was filled with a sense of sadness. Don't worry, Dimitri, she thought—I'm not about to tell you that I love you and that my heart will be broken the day you take your flight out of Heathrow. Even if she was beginning to suspect that it was true.

'It's about Zoe.'

His body language remained just as forbidding. This was not her territory and she had no right straying into it. 'What *about* Zoe?' he questioned repressively.

'Dimitri, she still thinks that you treat her like a child!' she blurted out. 'And I'm afraid that I agree with her.'

'Molly,' he said warningly.

She ignored the warning. And the flashing look of displeasure in his black eyes. 'I think you've got to understand that she's growing up. Fast.'

'I do not intend having this conversation—'

'Well, you're going to have it!' she retorted,

blanking the thunderous expression on his face, as if he couldn't believe that someone had just spoken to him like that. Maybe people didn't—and that couldn't be good, surely? 'She says that she isn't allowed enough say in matters, or enough freedom—'

'Freedom?' he echoed tightly.

'Yes, freedom! It's what teenagers crave—it's the loosening of the bonds which tie them—the thing which puts them on the road to independence!'

'The freedom for her to paint her face?' he roared. 'To behave like a tramp? To indulge in under-age sex...' He saw her face and stopped. 'Molly, I didn't mean—'

'Oh, please don't try to backtrack now!' she snapped and rose to her feet, her voice trembling with rage. 'You know exactly what you meant! And for your information, Dimitri—I was *not* under age when we first had sex! I was eighteen years old, young, yes—but it was legal! I hadn't planned it that way, but it's hardly a capital crime.' And she had loved him—but from the look on his face he didn't want to be reminded of *that*.

'Are you advocating free love for my daughter?' he questioned.

'Of course I'm not! She's only fifteen!'

'Exactly!' he thundered.

They glared at one another and Molly steadied herself. She wasn't exactly being much help to Zoe if she continued with a slanging match and started bringing her *own* feelings into it.

'Dimitri,' she said quietly. 'You know that the world has changed since we were young. Even on Pondiki.'

Yes, he knew that. 'I am not guilty of living in the Dark Ages, Molly—I simply want to protect my daughter.'

'Of course you do—but you can't wrap her up in cotton wool. You can just guide her and teach her your values and hope that she wants to emulate them.'

'You think that my values are worth teaching, then?'

There was a pause. 'Only you can answer that. But Zoe finds life on such a small island constricting. Surely you can see that.' She took a deep breath. 'She wants to be a model, you know.'

He shook his head as if she were mad. 'She wants to be a doctor,' he contradicted.

'Not any more. An agent who was on holiday on the island gave her a card and told her to call. A top New York agency. She thinks that she has what it takes, and Zoe wants to do it. Badly,' she finished.

He felt as though he had been slapped in the face. 'Who told you this?'

'She did, of course!'

'She has never once mentioned it to me!'

'No, of course she hasn't. She's scared to. She thinks that you will be upset because she no longer wants to do medicine.'

'I never said that!'

'Well, have you discussed the future with her? Lately?'

'She's too young to know what she really wants. If she no longer wants to be a doctor, then that is fine—but not modelling. No, not that.'

'She is *not* too young, Dimitri! She's going on sixteen, for heaven's sake! She's really very mature for her age—and that's hardly surprising considering the knocks she's had in her life!'

It occurred to him that this was really none of Molly's business, but she seemed to know more about his daughter's wants and needs than he did. Had he been guilty of wrapping her in cotton wool, as Molly had said?

Molly's courage was growing by the minute. She had nothing to lose—Dimitri would soon be gone from her life—and she owed this to Zoe. Maybe in a funny kind of way she owed it to Malantha, too.

'She loves you very much,' she said carefully. 'But feels she can't really talk to you—'

'The way she can with you, you mean?' he interjected silkily.

The silence which followed seemed to go on for an eternity. 'And just what is that supposed to mean?'

Dimitri's black eyes were like some hard, cold metal. 'It hasn't ever worked before, and it won't work this time,' he said obliquely.

'You're speaking in riddles, Dimitri,' she said, in a low voice. But she knew exactly what he was getting at. She just wanted him to say it aloud, knowing that when he did it would shatter everything they had ever shared, even the past. And perhaps that was best.

'Trying to inveigle your way into my life by whatever means it takes. Making yourself my daughter's confidante—and an invaluable one. I am not looking for another wife, Molly, and she is not looking for a substitute mother.'

She stood up to face him. 'And I'm not looking for another husband and even if I were…' she paused deliberately for effect, injecting the words with the meaning she really felt at that moment, as strongly as if it were tatooed onto her skin '…even if I were, it would not be you! A man stuck in the Dark Ages! A man who picks women up and then puts them down again as he would a cup of coffee!' She headed towards the door.

'Where do you think you are you going?' he demanded.

'Where do you think? To buy my trousseau?' she spat out sarcastically. 'I'm going downstairs while you finish dressing! And then you can get out!'

'Don't go!'

'Oh, no!' She shook her head. 'You can't talk to me like that and you can't stop me, either! I am not your possession, Dimitri, and neither is Zoe. Children are only loaned to you, you know—you have to learn to let them go!'

He took a deep, steadying breath. 'Have you quite finished?'

'No, I have not! Because I'll tell you something

else, Dimitri Nicharos! I *agreed* to become your
lover, and I must have needed my head examining!
You're just as bloody hotheaded and narrow-minded
as you ever were! You still see the world according
to *you*, and your prejudices—without bothering to
look at the whole picture!' She moved towards the
door.

'Do not walk out of here!'

She laughed, hearing the slight tinge of hysteria in
her voice. 'Why? Has no woman ever walked out on
you before?'

'No,' he said, without thinking.

Something inside her snapped. It wasn't just his
arrogance, though that was bad enough—it was his
tacit acknowledgement of the women who had gone
before her. Up until now she had accepted the knowledge of those women very calmly—she had had no
choice—but in the light of everything which had
been said, it just became too much to bear. Well, they
were welcome to him!

'Don't go,' he said again.

'Just watch me!'

She wrenched open the door but he had moved
across the room before she could make her escape
and she shook her head, her eyes wild and frightened—not of him, and what he would do. She knew
exactly what he would do—try to kiss her into sub-
mission, the way he knew he could. No, she was
frightened of her own reaction, of her body respond-
ing to him while her heart and her mind told her that
it was wrong. Disastrous.

'Don't you dare to lay a *finger* on me!'

'Molly, you are angry—'

'Damned *right* I'm angry!'

'And you have every right to be,' he said unexpectedly.

Molly blinked. 'I do?'

'Yes. You do.' There was a pause. 'I am sorry for the things I said, for the things I accused you of. Truly, truly sorry.'

She blinked. Dimitri sounding so *contrite*? It took the wind completely out of her sails.

'Do not leave, Molly,' he said again, very softly. 'Please.'

And a plea from Dimitri was about as subtly powerful as it was possible to be.

She leaned against the door and closed her eyes, composing herself before she opened them again.

'I was only trying to help,' she said.

He nodded. 'I know you were.' And he was a man unused to accepting help—from anyone. He had shouldered life and its burdens completely on his own, but now he recognised that Molly had no hidden agenda, other than telling him something which his daughter had felt unable to tell him herself. 'I know you were,' he said softly, and put his arms around her.

'Please, don't—'

'You don't mean that,' he murmured.

No, she didn't. Molly closed her eyes against his shoulder. This felt close, closer almost than any other time she had been with him. Safe and warm and secure in his arms. She relaxed into his big, strong body for a moment, and then pulled away. Because the haven he represented was just an illusion.

'We'd better go, hadn't we? Zoe will be home soon.'

'We have a little while yet.' He ran a reflective fingertip down the side of her face. 'And I don't want to go. Not yet.'

How could such a simple action have such a profound effect? Just a whisper of a touch could have her trembling. 'Dimitri—'

'What?' His lips followed the path of his fingertip and Molly shuddered. 'What is it?'

She wanted to say that making love wouldn't solve anything—but then, Dimitri probably didn't think that there was anything to solve. She wanted to say that they had only just made love and that every time they did it brought her closer and closer to him in a way which she knew in her heart spelt danger.

His mouth reached her lips and she didn't resist—couldn't, and didn't want to resist, if the truth be known. And she wound her arms around his neck, the gesture telling him tacitly that, yes, she wanted him, too. This might be the last time. She bit her lip. There was to be a farewell lunch tomorrow, with Zoe too, and then he was flying home. And that would be that. She would probably never see him again.

Is this the last time? she wondered desperately.

He led her back to the bed and his expression was almost tender as he began to unbutton her dress once more, his lips anointing kisses onto her aching flesh and driving all rational thought away.

Except for one. That this was a little like a savings account—like putting money away for a rainy day. Each time that Dimitri made love to her it would be something to remember him by.

After he'd gone.

Rather fittingly, there was a grey and relentless drizzle as Zoe clambered into the back of the taxi with the suitcases, which just left Molly and Dimitri standing on the pavement. The lunch had been fine, if a little on the superficial side. Nothing had been said about medicine, or modelling, for which Molly was inordinately grateful. She didn't want to spoil the day or her memories with an atmosphere—and she was grateful for Zoe's presence, too. Having her there meant that things were kept light and breezy. Lots of things were said, but nothing of any significance.

Molly took a deep breath. 'So.'

'So.' Dimitri smiled. 'It has been wonderful, Molly.'

'Yes.'

They looked at each other and he felt a frustrated sense of longing that he could not kiss her as he really wanted to kiss her. His daughter might like Molly, might know about their affair on some subconscious level, but knowing that something was happening in theory was a little bit different from actually seeing it acted out in front of you.

So he contented himself with a swift kiss. Or rather, the swift kiss left him feeling distinctly *dis*contented.

Next time he came to England—and maybe it would be sooner than he had originally planned—then he would come alone. Though of course, by then Molly might have someone else...but that was a risk he would just have to take.

His eyes imprisoned her in a glittering ebony blaze.

'Goodbye, Molly,' he murmured. 'I'll ring you.' He hesitated, knowing that his next choice of word was important. If he said 'some time' it would mean never and if he said 'tomorrow' it would commit him to something he was not sure he wanted to commit to. 'Soon,' he added. 'Okay?'

'Okay.' She wasn't going to count on it, but she nodded anyway, and gave him a bright, grown-up smile. 'Goodbye, Dimitri,' she managed. 'Safe journey.'

She watched the tail-lights of the taxi retreating, and Zoe waving through the back window, and Dimitri beside her, his handsome face thrown into shadowed relief, so that it was impossible to read his expression.

Funny. They said that sorry was the hardest word to say, but saying goodbye to someone you loved had to come a close second.

CHAPTER TEN

MOLLY waited for Dimitri to ring, telling herself that she wasn't waiting at all. That she needed to be around the house—and then she found a good reason to be, because she started decorating the sitting room in dramatic shades of blue and grey. As if she wanted to change the externals in her life, to match the changes which had taken place inside, although she took care not to analyse *those* too much. Close scrutiny of her feelings might bring her to the conclusion that the love she had felt for Dimitri had been reborn in a new and rather terrifying form.

She spoke to her editor on the phone and agreed that she would fly out to Paris at the end of the month to start her new book. And she told herself that if he hadn't rung after three days, then he wouldn't ring at all, and even if he did she would be as cool as a cucumber.

So that every time the phone rang she deliberately counted to seven before she answered it. Until...

'Molly Garcia.'

'Mol-ly?'

A few days could seem like an eternity when you were waiting, and she seemed to have been waiting for so long to hear the rich, deep voice that now she finally had, it threw her. 'H-hello?'

'It's Dimitri.'

'Dimitri.' Deep breath. Take it easy. Don't show him how much this means. 'How are you?'

He thought of the long, aching nights. 'I miss you.'

She swallowed. 'You *do*?'

'Don't you miss me?'

Did she miss him? Oh, yes—she missed him all right. How was it possible to miss a man so much—when, up until a few short weeks ago she had consigned him firmly to memory?

'A little,' she murmured, and that *wasn't* being hypocritical—it was simply protecting herself.

'Only a little?'

'Mmm. I've been busy.'

'Oh.'

She thought he sounded—if not disappointed, then a little surprised. 'Think I've been crying into my pillow every night, do you, Dimitri?' she teased.

'Well, if you haven't been crying, what else have you been doing at night, Molly?' he purred. 'Shall I tell you what I've been doing?'

She blushed, even though he was thousands of miles away. 'Stop it.'

'Last night I dreamt that I was running my hands all over your body, Molly, and when I awoke…'

His voice had tailed off to a silky and suggestive whisper, and Molly knew exactly what he was doing. Or trying to do.

'I'm not having phone-sex with you, if that's what you're thinking!' she said crisply.

Her schoolmistressy tone was like having a bucket

of cold water tipped all over him, and as the ache subsided Dimitri gave a low laugh of pleasure. Did he really imagine that Molly would settle for dirty talk over the telephone?

He rubbed the back of his neck and yawned. 'So tell me what you have been so busy doing?'

'Oh, I've been painting the sitting room.'

'Mmm? Anything else?'

'And making travel plans for the next book.'

'In Paris?'

'That's right.'

'So when do you go to Paris?'

'At the end of the month.'

He did a hasty calculation in his head. 'And will you be too busy to see me?'

Her heart leapt with excitement and she cursed it. Some things you had no control over—like your body's reaction—but some things you did. Like your voice, and now she kept hers calm. 'I didn't think that was an option.'

'There is always an option,' he returned. 'How about if I meet you there?'

'Where? In Paris?'

'Why not?'

Her heart raced. 'Just like that? You can take another holiday when you've only just got back?'

'Not a holiday,' he answered quickly. 'You will be working and therefore I will be working, too.'

'But won't they mind you being away from the hotel again, so soon?'

'Do not concern yourself with that. Think instead of Paris…and all the fun we can have together.'

'Okay,' she said lightly, as if it didn't matter to her one way or the other. 'I'll meet you in Paris.'

'I'll book us a hotel.'

The thought of spending a night with him—a whole night—made her dizzy with desire, but… 'No, Dimitri,' she said softly. '*I'll* book the hotel.'

'Is this a replay of the restaurant bill?' he questioned wryly. 'An attempt to show me how independent you are?'

'Not at all. This is strictly business, not personal— and hotels are my business.'

'They're mine as well,' he pointed out, in an amused voice.

'But the whole point of me going to France is to research places for women to stay, whereas I assume you aren't planning to uproot a hotel and have it flown wholesale back to Pondiki?'

He laughed. 'So you're going to subject me to a place all pink and frilly?' he suggested sardonically.

'That may be *your* perception of what women like,' she laughed. 'But if it is, then I'm afraid you're way off the mark. Women these days want comfort and value for money.'

'And what else do women want, Molly?' he questioned softly.

She felt more confident now. 'I'll show you,' she promised.

'I can hardly wait.'

Neither could she. Never had a business trip held

more allure for her. He was there waiting for her at
Charles de Gaulle, tall and striking, his black hair
gleaming ebony beneath the airport lights, his narrowed eyes glittering with anticipation as she walked
towards him, only just stopping herself from running
and hurling herself into his arms.

But she was a woman in her thirties, she reminded
herself as she had done again and again, and that was
not how women her age should behave. She had told
him that she would make her own way to the hotel,
but he had insisted on meeting her—and wasn't there
a stupid, feminine part of her that had *liked* him in-
sisting, for all her protestations? Maybe, deep down,
there was a part of every woman who liked a strong,
dominant man, for all their hard-earned independence.

He watched her approach, thinking how the years
had changed her. All the passion and the exuberance
which had been so much part of her had now been
contained and channelled into this coolly beautiful
creature with her pale blonde hair and her icy blue
eyes which matched her sun-dress. Oh, she still had
passion—that much was not in doubt—but she only
displayed it when he was making love to her.

Which should have made things perfect. Dimitri
did not like overt and possessive displays of affection
from his women, particularly in public. So why was
he left wanting to shatter that calm demeanour of
hers? Was it simply a case of wanting what he hadn't
got? He was used to women who idolised him and
put him on a pedestal and once Molly had been

among their number, but then, he too had felt the same way about her.

But putting people on a pedestal was dangerous. It was such a lonely place to be and who could blame them if they fell?

'Hello,' she said, and wishing that this awful, inexplicable *shyness* would leave her. 'You didn't have to meet me, you know.'

'So you told me,' he said drily, and smiled. 'But here I am, and here you are—so let us waste no more time talking about it. Shall we go?'

No kiss, then.

'Let's.'

In the taxi, she turned to him. 'How's Zoe.'

'She is well.'

She didn't ask and therefore he felt free to tell her. 'The ongoing discussions about her future continue.'

She gave him a coolly curious look. 'And?'

He shrugged. 'She seems to be wearing me down.'

Molly hid a smile. It seemed that Dimitri was learning that he would never be truly happy unless his daughter followed her own dreams.

'You seem to have given her the courage to stand up for what she wants,' he commented ruefully.

'Good!'

'Fighting words, Molly,' he murmured, and ran a reflective finger over the outline of her lips, feeling the instinctive tremble his touch provoked. 'Will you fight me later, *agape mou*?'

'I…I hope I won't need to,' she said shakily. If there was any fighting to be done, it was with herself—telling herself to accept this for what it was, and not for what she wanted it to be. And if she were being practical, she knew in her heart that it could never be any more than this. There had been very good reasons why it had not worked before—even if you discounted their age—and nothing had fundamentally changed.

Their lives were still too different. And, yes, the relationship was now running over his original timescale, but she would be mad to think he would ever marry her.

She turned her face to blindly look out of the window, appalled at the direction of her thoughts. A weekend in Paris and she was thinking *marriage*? How appalled would *he* be?

'We're here,' he said quietly, wondering what had caused her to move away from him like that.

In the suite they stood facing each other.

'What is it?' he asked, frowning.

'I'm supposed to be making notes on everything,' she said.

'You want to?'

'No,' she said, rather desperately.

He smiled. 'What do you want to do, then?'

'This.' She walked over to him, put her arms around his neck and kissed him, with a kiss that was deep and sweet and right.

He lifted his head, dazed by the power of it. 'Molly,' he said simply.

He undressed her. Slowly, almost tenderly, and then undressed himself and when they were both naked, on a bed and in a room which Molly had barely registered, he began to kiss her. To kiss her as if he never wanted to stop kissing her.

She opened her mouth to him as her eyes fluttered to a close, pulled his warm, hard body against hers and, moments later, into hers. And with each exquisite thrust, she gave a helpless little cry which soon—almost too soon—became a sound which was a mixture of sobbed fulfilment and an aching kind of regret.

He moaned her name, felt the world recede, and when his senses began their stealthy pulse back to something which resembled normality he felt the slick sheen of her tears against his shoulder and lifted her head, staring at her wet eyes with a frown.

'Tears, Molly?' he questioned sombrely.

If she wasn't careful she would blow everything with an over-the-top display of emotion.

She gave a smile and dropped a kiss on his parted lips. 'Sorry.'

'Why are you crying?'

She wiped them away. Don't go there, Dimitri. 'Oh, it's just a woman thing.'

'Tell me.'

She shook her head. 'Sorry—no can do!' She gave him a mock-stern look. 'We are creatures of mystery, didn't you know? Men don't understand us, that's what makes us so alluring.' She moved away from him, sat up and gazed round the room. 'Nice room,' she remarked.

'Mmm.' But he wasn't looking at the room. 'What do you want to do now?'

She would have liked to have spent the rest of the evening in bed with him and made love with him over and over again until they were both spent and fell into an exhausted and sated sleep. In fact, she wouldn't have given a damn if they didn't set foot outside the suite for the duration of their stay—but that wasn't why she was here. And that kind of behaviour was not only non-productive—it was extremely dangerous, too. She had a job and a living to earn. A life to lead, of which Dimitri was only a tiny, tiny part.

'I have a list of bars we should visit,' she said. 'And a restaurant I'd like to give a whirl. How does that sound to you?'

It sounded hell, if the truth be known. 'Fine,' he said flatly.

They put their clothes back on in silence, and Molly thought sometimes the act of getting dressed could be more intimate than getting undressed. Once the fires of passion had burnt out, there remained nothing but cold, harsh reality—and this reality suddenly felt very cold indeed. And it was intimate only in so much as the fact that she was putting on her underwear in front of him—a false intimacy, in fact—for there were no shared looks, or giggles or jokes or any of the accompanying things which would have occurred if they truly *were* a couple.

She pulled her sleek black jersey dress over her head, brushed out her hair and slid on a pair of high-heeled shoes which wouldn't normally have been her number one choice for sightseeing, but hell—surely this was work *and* pleasure?

Dimitri finished fastening his cuff-links and glanced up at her, his eyes as shuttered as his brief smile.

'Ready?'

'Sure.'

But Paris somehow managed to weave its subtle magic, despite the fact that she dragged him to four different bars where he moodily drank mineral water in each. Because only when they were seated face to face in a restaurant close to the Champs-Elysées and had been handed menus the size of large atlases did Dimitri allow his lips to break into a slow smile.

'You have exhausted me, *agape*,' he murmured.

She looked up from behind the menu, raising her eyebrows. 'After only once? Shame on you, Dimitri!' she teased. 'Why, in the old days you wouldn't have let me out of your arms.'

'That's because in the old days you wouldn't have wanted to!'

'No, well.' The French words danced unintelligibly on the page before her. 'Things change.'

'Do you wish they didn't?' he asked suddenly.

She put her menu down. This was deep, coming from him, and the expression in his eyes cautioned her not to be flippant. There was a time for flippancy, and it was definitely not now.

'Well, of course I do! Sometimes.' She drew a deep breath and let the words tumble out. 'There's a silly, romantic side to every woman who wishes that her first love could have worked out and that they had lived together, happily ever after.'

'But you think that's impossible?' he guessed.

She nodded. 'In ninety-nine point nine of all cases, yes—and very definitely in ours.'

He put his menu down. He had eaten little, but the food held no interest for him.

'And now?' he questioned softly.

It was one of those key questions—give the wrong answer and everything would be lost. She suspected that he was testing the ground, to find out just how serious she was and that if she came over as serious, then he would run as fast as he could in the opposite direction.

'I've learned not to look ahead,' she said slowly. 'Or to look back—there's no point, is there?'

He smiled. 'You mean live for today.'

She nodded, and, although it hurt her to say it, she knew that she must. Before he did. 'Yes. Because today is all we have, Dimitri.' All they would ever have. And after this weekend was over, they would each go back to their very different lives. She would have to learn to compartmentalise, just as he did, as all men did—otherwise she would be one of those women who yearned for the impossible, and the relationship—if you could call it that—simply would not survive.

'Shall we order?' she asked brightly.

'You order for me.'

'Me?' she squeaked.

'Sure. You're the one who has been studying the menu.'

Or giving the appearance of it. 'What do you fancy?'

He leaned forward, and beckoned her towards him, planted a kiss that lingered on her lips for far longer than it should have done, considering that they were in the window table of a restaurant, completely exposed to passers-by and other diners. But this *was* Paris—and Paris never frowned on lovers.

She closed her eyes briefly and drew away from the sensual invitation of his mouth. 'You—you...taste of sex,' she said weakly.

'I know. So do you. What was it that you asked me, *agape*?'

'I asked what you wanted to eat.'

'You,' he answered simply, and smiled at her look of shock and delight. 'Don't you know that in Greece we eat the women and the chicken with our fingers?'

'Dimitri.' She swallowed. 'I'm supposed to be reviewing this restaurant, and you're making it very difficult for me.'

'I know.' He pushed his menu away. 'Shall we go?'

'But we haven't eaten anything!'

'So?'

She put up one last, half-hearted fight. 'You'll be hungry later,' she warned.

'There's always room service.' His eyes flashed a stark black challenge. 'Come on, let's get your coat.'

She pushed her chair back. 'You're too used to

getting your own way,' she accused, and he laughed in response.

'Yes,' he agreed silkily. 'But we both know that what I want is what you want, too. You just wanted me to show you how much.'

She couldn't think of an answer, but then any rational thought was proving very difficult indeed. Other than the one glorious realisation that they were going back to the hotel for the night. *For the night.*

'You do realise that this is the very first time we've ever slept together?' she asked.

His face looked almost sad. 'Don't you know that I've thought of nothing else all evening?'

And then the taxi came.

CHAPTER ELEVEN

THE moon hung low over the sea, like a giant silver disc suspended in the dark sky by an invisible thread, and the reflection on the calm water was almost as bright as the moon itself.

Molly sighed. 'It's so beautiful, isn't it?'

But Dimitri didn't answer. She turned to him, seeing his profile as unmoving as if it had been carved from one of the rocks on which they sat, having just had dinner in a glorious open-air terrace restaurant just behind them.

The sounds of diners drifted out towards them, as did the faint burst of accordion music somewhere in the distance. She had thought that it had been a perfect evening, but Dimitri had seemed…distracted, almost. Not like him at all, though then she was forced to ask herself—how much or how well did she know him? Or he her?

Their relationship had continued—despite her fears that it would not—for just over a year since he and Zoe had left London. An exciting relationship—certainly as far as her friends were concerned. As Alison had said, what could be more perfect than meeting a man like Dimitri for wild weekends of uninhibited sex in some of the most beautiful cities in the world?

'You've got all the best parts of a relationship with a man, without all the dreary everyday things,' she had remarked. 'I tell you, if I never had to wash another shirt again or go hunting for that elusive stray sock, then I would be a very happy woman indeed.'

And Molly had laughed, and agreed.

But nothing in life was that simple, was it? She saw the best bits of Dimitri, true—so was it just something perverse and contrary in the female psyche which made her long for the other, normal, everyday bits, too? Not that she would ever be enamoured of hunting for his socks, of course. For a start, she knew he never wore any when he was on Pondiki, but as going there was never likely to be an option, then she wasn't likely to get the opportunity.

But she sometimes found herself longing wistfully to rub the strain away from his temples when he had had a long, hard day and then she found herself wondering whether that was just a sublimated maternal instinct.

Because, of course, there was the subject of children, too. Not with Dimitri—he already had his family, in Zoe, and she couldn't really see him wanting another one, not with his daughter going on seventeen and soon to fly the nest. But Molly's biological clock was ticking away relentlessly. If she wanted children she couldn't wait for ever.

And Dimitri had shown no sign of wanting to commit; she had never expected him to—but the fact remained that if she wanted children, then she was going to have to find a man to father them. Which meant falling in love with someone, and that was never likely to happen while she stayed with Dimitri.

Yet she couldn't bear the thought of letting him go. Catch-22, or what?

Sometimes she thought about it, telling herself that she was wasting her time with him—but could the intense pleasure she experienced in his company ever be described as time-wasting? If she tried broaching the subject with him, of suggesting that they both might like the freedom to look elsewhere—him for a suitable wife who could live with him on Pondiki and her for a potential father to a child she might one day have—then wouldn't that have the air of the ultimatum about it? And didn't he just loathe those? She had seen his reaction when she had brought up the subject of Zoe—he had imagined that she was pushing him into a corner, and his instinct had been to flee.

No, all things considered, she was content enough with what she had.

'Dimitri?'

He stirred himself from his thoughts, lapsing automatically into Greek, as he sometimes did when he was distracted. *'Ne?'*

She never knew what he was thinking, but then, when did she ever ask—and risk getting answers she did not want? No, it was easier this way. Light and loving—in the way that loving could be if it was never declared. Though she was only sure of her own feelings, not his, because Dimitri had never told her

that he loved her—not in a year of meeting and trav-
elling together. Of being, to all intents and purposes—a couple. She told herself that she was glad.
Glad that he wasn't saying things he didn't mean,
just to please her, but maybe that was because he
was a sensible and pragmatic man.

Once you said those three words which shouldn't
mean as much as they always did, well, then—things
changed. Inevitably.

People started getting ideas and expectations.
Declared love seemed to involve some kind of commitment to the future and that didn't fit in with either
of their lives. Well, it certainly didn't fit in with
Dimitri's—he had told her that, a long time ago—
and what had happened to make him change his
mind?

A couple could go on for years having just the
kind of relationship as theirs—until, she supposed,
one of them tired of it. Or until someone else came
along... The shirt-washing and sock-hunting scenario often destroyed a romance—and romance was
what they had. People put a high price on romance,
they chased it and yearned for it. Now that she had
it—she mustn't knock it.

'What did you say?' he questioned.

It was the kind of question which sounded inane
when you repeated it. 'I just said that it was beautiful.
It is, isn't it?'

'Very,' he said flatly.

She felt the first intimations of unease. He had
definitely been in a preoccupied mood, now she

thought about it—ever since she had met him at the airport. Now that Zoe was older, he was able to make their meetings more frequent, and yet over the past couple of months she'd suspected that something was driving a wedge between them.

Was he worried about leaving his hotel so much?

'And it was a lovely dinner,' she added, inconsequentially, as people did when they wanted to say something, but couldn't really think what to say.

'Lovely,' he agreed, still with that odd, flat note in his voice. 'Lovely dinner, lovely hotel, lovely view.'

The dark profile was still gazing out to sea.

'What's the matter?' she asked suddenly, and as soon as she asked it she knew that she had placed herself in a vulnerable position. An open question like that might mean he might tell her. Tell her what? That their affair had also been 'lovely' but now it was over?

He turned then and his eyes were glittering as brightly as the moon, but their message as enigmatic as the moon itself. 'Shall we go for a walk, *agape*?' he questioned softly.

It sounded like more than a simple invitation to do just that. It sounded…not exactly threatening, but filling her with a faint sense of foreboding. Molly looked down at the strappy silver shoes she wore, expensive designer shoes which matched the silver dress. Her heart was beating very fast. The palms of her hands were clammy, and it wasn't just the hot, balmy Mediterranean air. No, there was some un-

known and steely quality to Dimitri tonight and suddenly she knew that whatever he had to tell her might
be easier heard if they were walking side by side by
a seashore.

'Sure,' she agreed, kicked off her shoes and picked
them up. They were not as equal as she had thought
they were, she realised. If they had been then she
would have fixed him with a direct stare and asked
him what he wanted to say. And she would have
shruggingly accepted it whatever it was. So what had
happened to the cool, calm woman who had decided
that this was a grown-up affair and that she would
regard it as that, nothing more and nothing less?

She had fallen in love and left her by the wayside,
she realised. And like all women in love with a man
who did not reciprocate the emotion, she walked on
eggshells, even if she weren't aware that she were
doing so.

Until now.

She watched silently as Dimitri took off his own
shoes and socks and rolled up his trousers, leaving
those luscious dark-skinned ankles bare. Then he
jumped down onto the sand and held his arms up to
catch her, but she shook her head and jumped down.
Independently.

It might just be a good idea to remember what that
felt like.

Because she also realised that although, to all intents and purposes, her life *was* independent—emo-
tionally she had come to rely on him a great deal.
No, more than that. To fulfil all her emotional

needs—and most of that fulfilment was purely fantasy. Because a man couldn't fill all your emotional needs if you only saw him once a month, could he? Even if that time together *was* pretty close to perfect; of course, it was going to be perfect—fantasy always was.

'Are you happy like this?' he demanded suddenly, as they came across a secluded, half-hidden stretch of sand.

Here it came. 'What, you mean right now?' she prevaricated.

'Mol-ly,' he growled and came to a halt, catching her into his arms and staring down at her, his face as stern as she had ever seen it. 'Why do you always play such flippant games with me?'

Because the alternative to playing games was the truth game, and Molly had never been quite so frightened of the truth as she was right then. 'Was I?'

He gave a grim kind of smile. 'You know damned well you were,' he said softly. 'I asked were you happy?'

'Of course.'

'You are?'

'Well, aren't you?'

Dimitri sighed. 'I thought that this would be perfect,' he said.

'What?'

What kind of a relationship did he want with Molly? he asked himself. An honest one, surely?

'This.' He shrugged. 'Us.'

'So it's not?' Fear ran in cool skitters over her

skin. 'That means you aren't happy,' she rushed on. 'Well, if you aren't, then it's best you tell me, best we finish it now, before one of us gets hurt.'

He raised his eyebrows. 'You want to finish it?'

For a moment she felt like a schoolgirl again, remembering the way she had ended an innocent relationship with a boy in her year because she had known, deep down, that it had been on its last legs and she had wanted to get in first. To salvage her pride.

But what she had with Dimitri went deeper than that, even if it was about to end. And she could not and would not lie about something as important as this, simply to salvage her pride.

'I've been thinking about it,' she said truthfully.

'Ah! And you want it to end?'

'Of course I don't!'

'Why not?'

'Well…well, because I like you.'

He nodded. He noted her careful use of the word. She really *had* been thinking. And so had he. 'And this—this life we have been living—it is enough for you?'

She thought of his sweet fluency with English and yet at that moment, he sounded very Greek. Looked very Greek, too, she thought with a little shiver of longing, but she suppressed it. Longing could get in the way of things sometimes. And hadn't she been suppressing other stuff, too? Like her feelings?

'It isn't proper living, is it?' she ventured.

'Tell me,' he urged softly.

Why her? What if she just poured out how she felt, and found that it was different for him?

'Why don't you?'

He shrugged. 'It is true, I am a little tired of it.'

'Tired of it?' So he *did* want to finish it!

'Aren't you?' he questioned seriously.

Again, she felt the icy chill of fear. 'I don't know whether ''tired'' is the word I would have used to describe it,' she said faintly.

'Perhaps it was a poor choice of word,' he continued thoughtfully. 'Maybe discontented.'

'With me?'

'No, not with you—with the way things are. Always the hotel rooms! Always the fancy restaurants!'

'What's wrong with them?'

He shook his head. His thoughts were spinning and, for once in his life, his words could not seem to keep up with them. 'They are not real. Are they?' he questioned, and she dropped her eyes to stare at the white sand which ridged up between her bare toes.

'No. They're not,' she whispered, and looked up at him. 'That's exactly what I was thinking.'

'It is as if we had sat down for a meal together and never got past the first course,' he mused. He stared at her. 'Do you want to come back to Pondiki with me?'

Her heart pounded. She must be very careful not to leap in with both feet. 'You mean for a holiday?'

'Of course. I'm not about to get you your old job back in the taverna!'

Which hadn't been what she had meant at all.

'Would you like that?' he asked.

A holiday, that was all he was offering her, but even so, it was a change, a step…she just wasn't sure in which direction. 'You don't think that it will in-cite…comment?'

'I would be astonished if it did not, wouldn't you?' he answered drily.

'And memories?'

But he shook his head. 'Not so many memories now, Molly. Time fades them away.' He looked down at the shoreline. 'Just like the waves washing away the sand.'

Molly wasn't so sure. 'Don't people have long memories?'

'Some, I guess—though many of the older gen-eration are dead now, of course.'

She heard the sadness in his voice. His mother had died last year. Another chapter closed. Things never remained the same. They couldn't. Life moved on.

'But where would we stay?' she questioned. 'In the hotel? Or maybe,' she put in quickly, 'maybe I wouldn't stay with you at all?'

He burst out laughing at this. 'This is supposed to be an enjoyable interlude,' he murmured. 'Not an endurance test!'

An interlude—well, *that* was an interesting word, too. 'Well, where then?'

He hesitated. 'On Petros. You remember Petros?'

Briefly, she closed her eyes. How could he even ask her a question like that? Of course she remembered Petros—the tiny sister island to Pondiki, which lay like a sleeping cat just to the west. On some days, it looked as though you could swim to it in a couple of minutes—though she knew that it was five miles away. And sometimes, when the rains came, it disappeared altogether—as if it had been a figment of the imagination all along. Like so many things...

Sometimes, when they had lain together beneath the sheltering rocks on the beach, their bodies warm and sandy and spent, they had stared across at the uninhabited mound.

'One day I will build a house there,' Dimitri had vowed, and Molly had rested her cheek against the faint stubble of his, and thought that it was just a pipedream.

'Of course I remember it. Why, is there a hotel there now?'

He shook his dark head. 'Not a hotel, no—I have a house there.'

Her eyes widened. 'You said you'd build one!'

'Ah! You *do* remember! Well, I did build one. It is very private and no one goes there but me and Zoe—though she finds it too quiet, now, of course. But that is as it should be,' he mused and looked at her. 'I have accepted, you see, that my daughter loves the bright lights of the city.'

'Doesn't mean that Petros won't always be her home—even if she doesn't actually live there.'

He smiled. 'Feminine logic! But, yes, I take your point.'

'And she's still set on modelling?'

'Hell-bent.'

'You don't mind?'

He gave a quick grimace. 'It would not have been my first choice of career for her, but if her heart is set on it, then who am I to oppose it? Better she does it with my blessing, for to alienate her would achieve nothing. At least this way she can turn to me for help if things do not turn out as planned. Come on—let's sit down.'

They sat side by side in the soft, cool sand and Dimitri glanced at her rucked up silver dress with amusement mixed in with a little lust. 'You're going to ruin that dress,' he remarked.

'It's only a dress—and if a dress can't withstand moonlit sand, then it doesn't deserve to be worn.'

'It doesn't deserve to be worn now,' he murmured.

'Shall I take it off?'

'In a minute. You'll distract me.'

'You're distracted already. You have been all evening.'

'I know. So when will you come?'

And suddenly she was afraid. Afraid of why he really wanted her to go. Was it some kind of test? To see if they were truly compatible? Two weeks on a deserted island would certainly tell you if that were the case.

'Zoe is visiting London with one of her aunts,' he

said slowly. 'She isn't back until next week. You could come now, if you like.'

She stared at him. 'When?'

He smiled as he slipped the bodice of her dress down, to discover that her breasts were completely bare beneath. 'Tomorrow. Fly back with me.'

'I don't have enough clothes for a holiday.'

'But you won't need many. Not on Petros.'

Now he was distracting *her*, with his fingers splaying possessively over her, heating and arousing her air-cooled flesh. 'O-okay,' she agreed shakily, and pulled him down onto the sand. 'I will.'

The tarmac was as hot and as blistering as she remembered, as was the heady mixture of lemon and pine which scented the air when Molly alighted from the plane. The warm wind from the engines whipped up her hair and she had to hang onto her straw hat.

Dimitri glanced at her. 'How does it feel?'

'Hot.' She glanced back at him. 'It feels strange,' she admitted. 'And beautiful,' she added, looking around.

It was as breathtaking as ever, this tiny Greek paradise. Mount Urlin still rose in the distance, mighty and magnificent—and further still she could see a sea so darkly blue that it looked almost black.

So much of what she remembered was the same, but there were differences, too. The airport terminal had been completely modernised and it now looked sparkling and spanking new and deliciously air-conditioned.

And she noticed that people stood up straighter as she and Dimitri were waved through customs and that people turned to look at him, a bit like the way women did at parties, only more so, and it was men, too.

'Why is everyone looking at you?' she asked.

'Because I'm so good-looking?'

'No, seriously.'

'Oh, I'm such an important man, Molly,' he murmured.

She wasn't sure whether or not he was joking. His family's hotel had been the best on the island—but she could not remember quite the same amount of deference all those years ago. Though maybe she hadn't noticed that kind of thing then. Teenagers weren't into status much, were they?

'There are more cars,' she observed wryly as she slid onto the seat of the smart silver car which was waiting outside for them.

'I know.' He shrugged. 'Such is the price of progress. But there are no cars on Petros,' he promised. 'I won't allow it.'

'You can't stop it, can you?'

He didn't answer, just spoke in rapid Greek to the driver as the car moved away. They drove slowly around the island, through Urlin Square, where the lemon trees were still draped with rainbow lanterns which would be lit when night-time fell. And past the taverna where Molly had once worked, and a little cry of nostalgia escaped from her lips.

'I wonder what Elena is doing now,' she said.

'I can tell you exactly what she is doing—she is living right there.' He pointed to a white house opposite. 'She helps her husband run the taverna, when she's not too busy with her four children.'

'Four!' commented Molly faintly.

'That's right. We can go and have lunch with her one day, if you'd like that,' he mentioned casually.

She turned to him. 'Oh, Dimitri, can we? I'd love that!' She frowned. 'But only if you think she'd like to see me?'

'I think she would like that just as much as you would,' he answered. 'Elena was very fond of you and she thought that I had behaved very badly towards you, as she told me at great length, after you'd gone.'

'Did she?'

'She did.'

'That must have taken a lot of courage on her part,' said Molly. 'She always seemed a little bit in awe of you.'

'Maybe it's that female bonding thing you all seem to have,' he said drily.

She turned to him as the car moved towards the Urlin Road, remembering the night she had travelled out on her scooter to spy on him. Then the way had seemed never-ending and all she had been able to focus on were the potholes to be avoided and the pine cones scattered in her path. But today she just saw the incredible loveliness of the place. The peace and the quiet. The sense of completion and continuity.

She could understand Zoe's take on the place as restricting. She could see that someone her age might view the island as a bit of a prison. But Elena had stayed, and so had Dimitri. They had seen its beauty and seen it grounded in generations, repeating the same cycle of a life which fundamentally never changed. But then human nature never did.

She let out a little gasp when she saw his hotel, for it had grown. Not upwards, but outwards—with clusters of small, white bougainvillea-clad buildings nestling in the green hillside.

'Wow!' she murmured. 'Expansion!'

He sent her a frowning look of query. 'But it works, *ne*? It is not an ugly development?'

She shook her head. 'Not at all. It all looks as though it was meant to be there. Who designed it?'

'I did.'

Somehow she had known this. 'So you're an architect now?'

'An architect of my own destiny,' he responded, with a smile.

'And do your sisters know I'm coming?'

'Of course.' There was a pause. 'I thought we might have dinner with them one night. When Zoe's back.'

She turned to him. 'They won't mind?'

'They wouldn't dare,' he commented drily.

The car moved through lemon groves, acid-bright mixed with lush green and he opened the window so that she could catch their fragrance and she breathed it in.

'This isn't the quickest way to Petros, is it, Dimitri?'

He shook his head as the car drove down a steep road to where the sapphire-blue sweep of a bay awaited them, with a little boat bobbing there, and in the distance, Petros—clear and close enough to touch today. 'No, I brought you by the longer, more scenic route. Do you mind? Are you tired?'

'No. No, I'm not tired.'

On the contrary, she felt as though she had suddenly been brought to life. She stepped out of the car, welcoming the heat of the sun on her face. The air smelt so clean and so fresh, so sweet with natural scents. Only the drowsy, mechanical hum of the cicadas could be heard and the lapping of the waves against the sand.

She looked at the boat, gleaming cobalt and white in the crystal water. 'Is that how we're getting out there?'

'It's the only way out there.'

It looked a bit small. 'Sure it won't sink?'

He laughed. 'Not with just us two.' He gestured to the car. 'The cases will follow later.'

The motor roared into life and they sped over to the island. The house he had built was fashioned into the side of a rock, so that the back half was deliciously cool and shaded, while the vast sea-staring windows at the front meant that it was almost like being outside.

It was simply and sparsely furnished, more like a monastery than a house, she thought, but the simplicity did it justice—the view over the sea was decoration enough.

'Shall we go and have a drink on the terrace?' he asked.

'Sounds like heaven.'

'I hope so.'

It *was* heaven—almost too much so—for how was she ever going to be able to go back to her old life when she had tasted these simple, stunning pleasures with the man she loved?

Each morning they woke early and swam naked as the sun rose over the sea, gilding it with rose and gold, tingling their skin with its first soft rays, though the water was as warm as fresh milk.

They explored every inch of the small island and Dimitri pointed out all the plants and the tiny insects; he seemed to know everything there was to know about the place, almost as if it was part of him—which, of course, it was.

He caught her fish, and they drizzled it with oil and lemon and cooked it over a fire on the beach, drinking rich red wine and watching the stars come out and listening to the faint sound of the holiday-makers' merriment over on Pondiki.

One day he took her back across the water to lunch at Elena's house and the two of them fell into each other's arms, unashamedly nostalgic, while four brown-eyed children peeped out shyly from behind a flowered cotton curtain and gradually crept out.

'How long you are staying?' Elena asked, when Dimitri had gone to the kitchen to find a corkscrew.

Molly shrugged. 'Only a couple of weeks.'

There was a pause. 'And you still love him?'

'Elena!'

'You do.'

'Of course I do.'

'So?'

'So nothing.'

'But he has brought you here, Molly. Why?'

She didn't know, she didn't dare ask, for fear that questions would shatter the magic which clung to her skin like insubstantial stardust.

They would read and sleep and make love and the hours flowed like honey into one another. Sometimes Molly felt as if she had fallen into a dream, never to wake again, but she didn't want to wake—she wanted to go on living this dream for ever.

And then Zoe phoned. She was flying into Pondiki with her aunt.

'Good.' Dimitri nodded. 'She will be pleased to see you.'

She shot him a slightly worried look. 'Dimitri, does Zoe *know*? That I'm staying here with you?'

'I no longer have secrets, Molly,' he said slowly.

'And—' she drew a deep breath '—does she know that you and I were once lovers?'

He shook his head. 'I haven't told her,' he said. 'Not that. And I doubt that anyone else will. There are some things it is not necessary that she knows, but if she asks I will tell her the truth.'

'She will hate me.'

'Her mother did not hate you, so why should she?'

She stared at him. 'You mean, you discussed me? With Malantha?'

'Of course I did,' he answered gently. 'She understood,' he said, nodding slightly as if to reaffirm that to himself. 'She had always known about the other girls. She knew that was the way it was, but she also knew that one day I would return to her.'

His honesty was reassuring, but it gave her an insight into the fact that his marriage really had been a marriage, no matter how short, and that he had loved and confided in his wife. And Molly was glad.

'So was I...was I just another body to you, Dimitri?' she asked painfully.

'You insult me by asking that,' he answered quietly. 'You know you weren't.'

But he had stopped short of saying that he loved her then, just as he had never indicated that he loved her now. And maybe he didn't, even though sometimes he acted as if he did. But he was a man who kept his feelings locked away—look at his reaction when Malantha had died: he had kept all his grief bottled up. It all came down to that old thing whether it was important to hear someone say, 'I love you,' or whether you were prepared to accept what you had.

'She knew that you were different,' he added softly.

'And she accepted that, too?'

'It wasn't easy for her, and perhaps in my youthful arrogance I asked too much of her, but, yes, she accepted it.'

They sat in silence for a while, letting the past retreat again to its proper place.

'Do you want to come to the airport when I collect Zoe?' he asked eventually.

Molly shook her head. 'No. I've had you all to myself—you go to your daughter.' She smiled. 'She must be dying to see you.'

He gave her a brief, hard kiss. 'Thank you.'

In a year Zoe had changed almost out of all recognition. The adolescent had gone and she had become a woman, a head-turning woman—even more beautiful than Molly remembered.

She was fizzing over with excitement and the sight of Molly sitting in her father's house didn't seem to faze her in the slightest, she was too full of her own plans and dreams to bother about theirs.

'You see, Papa,' she was saying, once he had brought them chilled lemon juice out onto the terrace, 'I've changed my mind about modelling in New York!'

'You have?' he questioned casually.

Molly thought how much he had changed. How softer and more accepting of life he had become.

'Because London is where it is happening! And that's where I want to be! And Molly lives in London, doesn't she? Molly can keep her eye on me!' She beamed a huge smile. 'Papa arranged for me to see someone at an agency in London, and they were just so *sweet*!' Her big dark eyes were trained anxiously on Molly. 'You can be my chaperone if I come and live in London, can't you, Molly?'

Dimitri gave a slow smile. 'Ah! I was kind of hoping you might come to that conclusion yourself. It seems the ideal solution.' His eyes caught her in their soft black blaze. 'What do you say, Molly?'

And Molly suddenly felt sick.

He had planned the whole thing! Like some grandmaster moving the chess pieces around, only in this case the pieces were people! Arranging for Zoe to 'see' someone in London—because, of course, London was a safer bet than New York. London was nearer and *she* was in London, and he was confident that she would do anything for him. Molly who would walk to the ends of the earth if he asked her to. Stupid Molly.

Here she had been, thinking that Dimitri had brought her here with some kind of idea in mind for the future—*their* future. To see if they could be compatible for more than spaced-out weekends spent in fancy hotels. And they had been, or so she had thought.

But all the time she had been agonising over their future, and fretting about her body-clock and wondering about having children...well, Dimitri had obviously just been testing her out. To see whether she was a fit kind of person to keep her eye on his daughter!

So now what did she say? If she turned Zoe down, it would look as though she was holding out for something more—and there was no way she wanted anything more. What had Dimitri once said? That things should be given freely. Well, there was no way she was going to ask anything of *him*. And she liked Zoe. She couldn't, in her heart, turn her down—but at what cost to her *own* feelings?

'I'd have to discuss it with your father, Zoe,' she said slowly. 'But I can't see that there would be a problem with that.'

'Honestly?'

'Honestly,' she echoed faintly, and pushed her chair back. 'Well, I expect you've got lots to talk about so I think I'll go and take a shower before supper. Will you both excuse me?'

Dimitri stood up, frowning. Her face had gone as pale as the moon. 'Molly?' he questioned. 'Are you okay?'

She gave him a bright, brittle smile. 'Of course I am. I'll see you in a while.'

She only just made it to the shower room. At least in there she could lock the door. At least in there, her tears could be mingled with the streaming jets of water.

CHAPTER TWELVE

'MOLLY?'

She ignored it. The jets of water were so loud that she could quite reasonably say she hadn't heard him, couldn't she?

'Molly. Either you open this damned door or I will take it off at the hinges!'

She turned the water off. She believed him. There was something in the tone of his voice which left her in no doubt whatsoever that he meant it. She slicked her wet hair away from her face and wrapped herself in a towel, then went to open the door, registering the look of dark fury on his face.

His eyes flicked over her. 'Put something on,' he snapped, and turned his back to gaze out at the sea, as if he couldn't bear to watch.

She thought of defying him, but what would be the point? She was trapped. Trapped on a paradise island which had become a prison, with a man who didn't love her.

She pulled a cotton dress over her still-damp naked body. 'You can turn round now.' But when he did, she recoiled from the cold, hard look in his eyes.

'What was that all about?' he demanded.

Was he so dense he couldn't see? 'I wanted a shower.'

'You wanted to let me know in no uncertain terms that the idea of including my daughter in your life obviously appalls you!'

'Mightn't it be easier all round if you employed a *professional* chaperone!' she bit back. 'Or are you planning to put me on the payroll?'

And suddenly he understood. She was confused, just the way he had been. Frightened, too—just as he had been. And the tumult of coming to terms with the way he really felt came out in a simple statement. 'I was planning to make you my wife, actually. But chaperone seems a better word than stepmother, don't you think? That makes you sound like a wicked witch. Which sometimes, *agape mou*, you really are.'

Molly sat down on the bed. Had they blown it? Had *she* blown it? 'Was?' she questioned faintly and then pulled herself together. 'You don't have to marry me, Dimitri,' she said tonelessly. 'I'm happy to do what I can for your daughter.'

He sat down on the bed next to her and took her face between his hands. 'Molly,' he said simply. 'If I told you that I love you, would that make a difference?'

Her heart lurched. Her hands shook and so did her head. 'Not if you're just saying it to make me feel better.'

'You think I would say something as big as that if I didn't mean it?'

She stared at him suspiciously. No, she didn't, but she had to know. 'Just like that?'

He shook his head. 'No, not just like that.'

'Then why now? Why, today?'

He sighed. Maybe his timing hadn't been perfect, but timing had always seemed set to work against him, especially where Molly was concerned.

'I've loved you for a long time, Molly,' he said. 'But I needed to be sure. I needed to know that it wasn't just some kind of overpowering physical attraction between us—something which had been cut off in its prime and which we both just needed to work out of our system. Loving someone is always a risk, but it doesn't have to be an impetuous risk.'

She nodded. Willing to just listen, but then he had never really spoken like this before, had he? From his heart.

'I tried to tell myself that it would wear itself out. That what we had would fade with time. But it hasn't. It's just got stronger. And then I thought about what it would be like if we finished.' He shrugged and for the very first time she saw his vulnerability. 'I couldn't bear it. I knew, deep down, that if I met you again, that this thing we have between us would always be there. Overpowering. Neverending. Fate brought us back together, sweet, *agape mou*—and who are we to argue with fate?'

'But the differences still remain.' She forced herself to see reason. If risk this was, then it must be a considered one. For both of them. 'You still have your life here in Greece, while mine is London.'

'I know. But time has merged those differences. You can be happy on Petros—I have seen that—and

I can be happy in London. We can move between both places.'

'But your life is *here*, Dimitri! And Zoe is to be in London—how are you going to fix that?'

'But I can work from London, too.' He saw her uncomprehending look, and smiled. 'I am, you see, Molly, a very wealthy man.'

She nearly said, *Maybe by Greek standards*, but she stopped herself and he was smiling.

'Yes, by Greek standards,' he said softly. 'And by international standards, too.'

She gasped. 'Can you read my mind?'

'I don't need to.' He touched her cheek. 'It's all written in your face. You wear your emotions in your eyes, Molly, didn't you know that?'

'D-do I?' So much for hiding the way she felt about him!

'You do. That was the main reason why I refused to see you after I found you with the American. I knew that if I looked at you I would know whether or not you had been unfaithful to me, and I didn't want to know that. It was easier all round to think that you had. Otherwise I would never have been able to let you go.' At the time it had come as a blessed relief to him—to find a legitimate reason to stop something which had been hurtling way out of his control.

And suddenly she understood. At eighteen, the risk had been too great. To devastate his life and his plans on the strength of a summer romance with a foreign teenager who was just starting out, the way he had been—well, it would have been madness.

If Zoe came to them in a year or two and told them that she was going to throw everything in to live an unknown life with an unknown man in an unknown place, then wouldn't they do everything in their power to stop her?

She noticed how easy it was to think in terms of 'we'. 'Will you kiss me now?' she begged.

He shook his head. 'Not yet. Not until you're wearing my ring on your finger.'

'You mean I have to wait until we're married?'

'I was thinking more of engagement. A *short* engagement,' he added with a smile when he saw her aghast look. He stood up and went to the pocket of his jacket and took out a tiny box, extracting a ring from it which, even from across the room, glittered as brightly as any of the clear stars which hung over the island, and Molly blinked at it in disbelieving joy.

He sat down again and slid it on her finger.

'Oh, it fits,' she gulped. 'Perfectly.'

'Of course it does. I knew it would. I know every centimetre of you, Molly. I knew exactly how wide your finger.' He lifted it to his lips and nibbled it. 'How soft. And how very sweet. Now come here and kiss your fiancé properly.'

But, reluctantly, she drew away after a minute. Zoe was somewhere in the house, and there were still a couple of questions which needed to be answered.

'What would you say if I told you I wanted children?'

'I would say that I wanted them, too.'

'You *do*?'

'But of course. If we are blessed.'

'You're sure?'

'I am Greek,' he said simply. 'How many would you like, Molly? Three, four, five?'

'Oh, Dimitri,' she sighed.

He kissed her again, until she thought of something else.

'When you say *rich*.' The mammoth diamond sparkling on her finger bore testament to his claim, though Molly wouldn't have cared if he had sealed their union with a curtain ring. 'How come? I mean…I don't understand. I know you have the hotel and everything, but…?'

He touched the cold diamond thoughtfully, then looked at her. 'When Zoe was a baby I knew that I was going to have to change something in my life—that unless I was less hands-on in the running of the hotel, I would never see her. I realised that Pondiki had a lot of resources which had not been tapped. I have an American friend, and he helped me get started. We began to manufacture the olives into oil—and then to export it.

'Pondiki oil is pretty special,' he said, unable to keep the pride from his voice. 'Prized among chefs all over the world. Next, our lemons were distilled, to make a rather potent liqueur.' He pulled a face. 'Not exactly to *my* taste, but it's very popular now, particularly in Germany.'

'Gosh,' said Molly faintly. 'Did you earn buckets?'

'Buckets,' he echoed, with a smile. 'It's another of the reasons I was, shall we say…*suspicious* of women. Avarice is a real turn-off and there are a lot of women out there who are drawn to men with big bank balances.'

'Oh, yeah?' she mocked. 'Nothing to do with your outrageous good looks, of course—or the fact that you're dynamite in bed?'

'Why, *agape mou*,' he murmured. 'You do say the sweetest things.'

But the thought of other women hurt. It had no right to, but it did.

He saw that, too. 'The other women are forgotten,' he said gently. 'There is only you. I don't let myself think of the other men in *your* life, Molly.'

'Well, you'd need a pretty fertile imagination to do that,' she said drily. 'Because there haven't been many, and no one since my husband. But you can wipe that look of smug satisfaction off your face and tell me about your semi-riches to real-riches story!'

He laughed. 'I ploughed the money back into the tourist industry. I bought up land—which meant that I could have control over what building went on. I wanted the island to retain its character,' he said. 'That was very important to me. Not to become crass and commercialised as so many places have done.'

'So you're King of Pondiki?' she teased.

'Mmm. But a benevolent one.' His eyes glittered. 'And I need a queen very badly.'

'Even an English one?'

'English, Greek, American—it wouldn't matter.'
His mouth softened and so did his voice. 'Just so
long as her name was Molly Garcia.'

EPILOGUE

'SHE looks beautiful, doesn't she?'

Dimitri flicked a glance at the glossy magazine and scowled. 'She looks all right.'

'Dimitri, she looks *beautiful*!' Molly thrust the magazine under his nose. 'Doesn't she?'

He stared down at the eight-page spread. Hard to believe that his little daughter—his baby—was cavorting across the Barbadian sand wearing a succession of what looked like torn sheets. And being paid an obscene amount of money to do it.

He nodded and a smile curved his mouth. 'Yes. She looks very beautiful,' he agreed softly. 'She is a very smart and successful young lady.'

Molly stretched. 'She rang last night when you were at the hotel. She wants to have a twenty-first party.'

'In New York?' he questioned wryly, since, despite all his machinations, his daughter had ended up living there anyway. Quite safely and sensibly, too, as it had turned out. In a stunning if over-priced loft apartment.

'No, here.' She stood up and went to massage the back of his neck. 'On Pondiki.'

He gave an almost imperceptible nod of approval,

but Molly saw it. 'What do you think?' she asked innocently.

'I'm happy to do it for her.' He wriggled a little as her fingers kneaded the stiff knot of muscle at the side of his neck. 'Mmm. That's good, Molly. Do it some more.'

'Shall I start to plan it with her, then?'

'Whatever you want, *agape*.' He sighed, but it was a blissful, happy sigh. 'You usually seem to get it, no matter what I say. Come here.' He pulled her round to sit on his lap.

'I thought you were enjoying that massage!' she protested.

'I was.' He gave the wicked, captivating smile which never failed to ensnare her. 'But it got me thinking of different, better ways to relax.'

'Oh?' She let him kiss her neck.

'Well, the boys are asleep.'

'And we don't know how long for,' she agreed.

'We could go and look in on them first,' he suggested. 'Just to check they're okay.'

'Any excuse!' she teased, but she loved him for his fierce devotion to *all* his children. She had given birth to the twins—twin boys which had driven the whole island into utter ecstasy and completely removed any lingering traces of resentment that anyone might still have felt for her. And Dimitri had more time this time around.

One day, she and Zoe had been watching him play in the water with them, patiently teaching the boisterous two-year-olds to swim.

Zoe had been paying one of her brief but frequent visits to the island, bringing in her wake hordes of paparazzi, which in turn had attracted the glitterati. Pondiki was in danger of becoming fashionable. Thank heavens that Dimitri had the control and the power not to let things get out of hand; not to lose the simple essence of the island, Molly had thought.

'Do you mind that your papa has more time to spend with them than he did with you?' she asked.

Zoe shook her long raven hair. 'Never. I'm so grateful for what he did for me. He changed his life to make mine better.'

'Yes.'

She had had the boys in London. Dimitri had suggested it and she had agreed to it readily, knowing the unspoken reason why. He did not want another wife airlifted by helicopter. In fact, he had been determinedly calm throughout her pregnancy, but she had seen the fear in his face sometimes, when he'd thought she hadn't been watching. And that was why she would not have any more children. They had enough. Their family and their happiness was perfect and complete.

After the birth, she had sold her big house in Hampstead, and bought a smaller one. She wanted to keep a base in London, for Zoe to use, and the boys when they were older, and for her and Dimitri. But she doubted she would ever live there again. She loved her Greek life too much, particularly now that she was halfway fluent in the language.

'Come on,' said Dimitri, and lifted her from his lap.

The two of them tiptoed along the corridor to the boys' room where their two black-haired boys were snuggled in adjoining cots, both sleeping the angelic sleep of the loved and the innocent.

Dimitri stared down at them, silent for a moment. 'It's hard to tell them apart when they're sleeping,' he admitted.

'But not when they're awake.'

'No.' Alexander was the bold adventurer—Lysander the quieter, more thoughtful of the two.

She watched while he smoothed down their glossy black curls, and Alexander stirred a little, while Lysander just slept on.

Dimitri said something in Greek.

'Goodnight, my sons,' whispered Molly and he turned to her and smiled.

Then he said something else, something soft and murmured which took much longer. 'Do you know what that means, Molly?'

She did.

He had just told her that she was his love, his life, his world. But she didn't need to understand Greek to know that. For as their love had grown, so had Dimitri learned to show it.

And these days she could read it in his eyes.

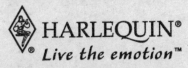

The world's bestselling romance series.

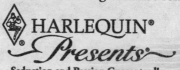

HARLEQUIN®
Presents

Seduction and Passion Guaranteed!

Your dream ticket to the vacation of a lifetime!

Why not relax and allow Harlequin Presents® to whisk you away
to stunning international locations with our new miniseries...

F♦REIGN AFFAIRS

*Where irresistible men and sophisticated women
surrender to seduction under the golden sun.*

Don't miss this opportunity to
experience glamorous lifestyles
and exotic settings in:

**Robyn Donald's
THE TEMPTRESS OF TARIKA BAY**
on sale July, #2336

THE FRENCH COUNT'S MISTRESS
by Susan Stephens
on sale August, #2342

THE SPANIARD'S WOMAN
by Diana Hamilton
on sale September, #2346

THE ITALIAN MARRIAGE
by Kathryn Ross
on sale October, #2353

FOREIGN AFFAIRS... A world full of passion!

Pick up a Harlequin Presents® novel and you will enter a world
of spine-tingling passion and provocative, tantalizing romance!

Available wherever Harlequin books are sold.

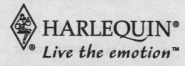

HARLEQUIN®
Live the emotion™

Visit us at www.eHarlequin.com

HPFAMA